Praise for
Just Like That

"Edgerton's got a story to tell you so get ready; it's coming at you fast. Get ready…"

—Linwood Barclay, international bestseller

"Edgerton draws memorable portraits of these dangerous and unpredictable characters."

—*Library Journal*

"*Just Like That* is yet another Les Edgerton winner. In his prison memoir, Edgerton conjures up in honest, Bukowski-esque prose a mad dog life lived behind and beyond the bars of institutional correctional facilities. Literature's version of Johnny Cash, America has yet another gifted bard to sing the blues of time served. I have long believed Edgerton to be an American original, who has for too long remained one of our best kept literary secrets."

—Cortright McMeel, author of *Short*

"*Just Like That* has it all. Great dialogue, whipcrack scenes and meaty characters haul you along on a hardboiled crime road-trip worthy of the Elmore Leonard and Joe R Lansdale. A shot to the heart as well as the head, *Just Like That* is highly recommended."

—Paul D. Brazill, author of *A Case of Noir*

"Edgerton establishes the kind convincing, and wrenching, interiority with his characters achieved by only the most adept fiction writers."

—Peter Donahue, Sam Houston State University

"This is good fiction; Edgerton writes lean and nasty prose."
—Dr. Francois Camoin, Director, Graduate
School of English, University of Utah

"Edgerton's best stories are uncompromising in their casual amorality. They stare you down over the barrel of a gun, rip you up whether or not the trigger gets squeezed."
—Diane Lefer, UCLA and Vermont College,
author of *The Circles I Move In*

"Les Edgerton creates a vivid and compelling world. We feel the rhythm of his language and live in the skins of his characters. Altogether, a memorable experience."
—Gladys Swan, Missouri University and
Vermont College, author of *A Visit to Stranger*

"Les Edgerton writes like a poet with a mean streak, and his prose goes down easy and smooth like good liquor as it carves up your insides."
—Henry Perez, bestselling author
of *Mourn the Living*

"There's no question the Edgerton loves to write...he does it so well!"
—Border's Bookstore Newsletter

"The characters in Edgerton's world bite down hard and grind up one another with their back teeth. Their authenticity is palpable as soft-shelled clams; these are sad, mean, fully human characters who long for connection almost as fiercely as they fear it."
—Melody Henion Stevenson, author
of *The Life Stone of Singing Bird*

JUST LIKE THAT

ALSO BY LES EDGERTON

The Genuine, Imitation, Plastic Kidnapping
The Rapist
The Bitch
Just Like That
Bomb! (formerly *The Perfect Crime*)
Mirror, Mirror
The Death of Tarpons

Short Story Collections
Monday's Meal (*)
Lagniappe

Writer's How-to Craft Books
Finding Your Voice
Hooked

Sports Books
Surviving Little League (Co-authored with son Mike when he was 12)
Perfect Game USA and the Future of Baseball

Other books on business, hairstyling, etc.

(*) Reissue forthcoming

LES EDGERTON

JUST LIKE THAT

Down & Out Books
3959 Van Dyke Rd, Ste. 265
Lutz, FL 33558
www.DownAndOutBooks.com

Cover design by JT Lindroos

ISBN: 1-946502-09-X
ISBN-13: 978-1-946502-09-4

*For my rap-partner Bud,
who not only provided much of the material in this book
from our real-life adventures, but who also saved my life back
in Pendleton more than once when my elephant mouth
overcame my hummingbird ass and he stood by me when
others took offense and made it clear that if anyone attacked
one of us, they were also taking on the other.*

For the loves of my life—Mary, Britney, Sienna and Mike.

*And, last but not least—for my readers; without readers,
writing is like having sex with yourself: The feedback you get
for your performance is ultimately flawed.*

FOREWORD

Parts of this novel have already seen publication as short stories in various publications, including *Murdaland, Flatmancrooked, Kansas Quarterly/Arkansas Review, High Plains Literary Review,* Houghton-Mifflin's *Best American Mystery Stories 2001,* and *Noir Nation.* A couple of the stories taken from this novel were nominated for the Pushcart Prize

It's largely autobiographical—perhaps eighty-five percent taken from my own life. It's centered around a road trip that I actually took with a friend from the joint—actually a couple of trips we made.

Awhile after I was released on parole from Pendleton, after serving a couple of years on a two-to-five-year sentence for second-degree burglary (plea-bargained down from eighty-two counts of second-degree burglary, one count of armed robbery, two counts of strong-arm robbery, and one count of possession with intent to deal), I was working in a barbershop in Lakeville, Indiana, for a guy named Dean. His shop was cleverly named "Dean's Barbershop." Dean was a truly cool guy and I loved working for him. At the time, I was charging a dollar a haircut; at the end of my journey as a stylist, I was charging one hundred dollars per cut.

Every single morning when I arrived at work, before we opened the doors, Dean always said the same thing over our morning coffee: "Les," he'd say, a faraway look in his eyes, "do you ever think when driving to work that someday you'd just like to keep going until you run out of gas, and then, wherever that is, you get a job there and live there?" I admitted that I had had the same thought many times myself. After all, until I was about forty, I'd never lived in one place more than two years. Some places I'd lived in more than once, but never for more than a two-year stretch. I loved moving to new places, and even today, after two years in one place, I find myself incredibly bored. Although...I've been stuck here in Fort Hooterville for many years.

Anyway, Dean never followed his own dream, but one day, I did just that. Was on my way to work and hadn't even thought about it when I woke up that morning, but halfway to Dean's it struck me that, yeah, I'd like to keep driving until I ran out of gas.

So I did just that. I pulled over, got on the phone and called Bud, a friend of mine from the joint who also was out. Like many ex-cons, Bud was of the same mind as I—that "rolling stone" mentality, and in a nanosecond, he said, "You bet. Give me half an hour and I'm with you."

An hour later, we were on our way. We would have left sooner but I had to stop to pick up some cash...at a convenience store. (Which I can talk about, as the statute of limitations is past for what transpired there. While most of the things in the book are true, I've presented them as fiction, mostly because of that pesky statute of limitations thing.)

Where to, neither of us had a clue. I just wanted to go somewhere warm and interesting, and to me, that meant South.

We ended up in Lake Charles, Louisiana, after some adventures along the way in Kentucky and New Orleans. Bud ended up climbing on a Trailways after a week or so to go back home to his girlfriend. I stayed awhile longer, and eventually, I also went back to Indiana.

I could never understand the big deal about leaving a place and moving to another. At least in those days, you couldn't move anywhere in the U.S. where you weren't a hundred dollars from home, wherever home was. That was the most Greyhound charged for a one-way ticket to anywhere in the country. That means that if the worst thing happened—you couldn't get a job, ran out of money, whatever—you were only a hundred bucks away from getting to where you had a support system and friends or family. And, no matter how broke a person might be, when push comes to shove, you can always come up with a hundred bucks.

To make this work as a novel, I had to take some liberties with the time line. Actually, I took two trips (with a different buddy) and have kind of combined them into one. One trip was a bike trip where another friend and I decided to take off on our bikes and go to Mexico. We never made it, but some of the things we did and experienced on that trip are included in *Just Like That*. One thing I left out is that at the time (of the bike trip), I had hair down to my waist and a long ZZ Top-kind of beard (this was before ZZ, or at least before I was aware of them.). We arrived at the Grand Canyon and there were these little places where you could pull your vehicle off the road and gaze down into the Canyon, and we were pulled off, toking on a joint and drinking some brewskies, when four RVs pulled over and all these "popcorners" (*) started piling out of their campers with their cameras and taking pictures. Only...they weren't taking pictures of the Grand Canyon. They were taking pictures of us! That's when I first shaved my head and cut off my beard (long before Michael Jordan!). Just too much...tourists taking my picture over the Grand Canyon.

A lot of this novel takes place in the joint at Pendleton and is based on experiences I had there. Most books written about the joint get most of it wrong. The reason is most folks who find themselves in prison are barely literate and not likely to write a book about their experiences. At least not the ones who find themselves in state joints. In federal joints, it's a bit different, as they house white-collar criminals, but then most federal joints aren't anything like state joints. If I ever think I'm going to end up in a state joint again, I'm pulling a federal crime and 'fessing up to that so that I go to Prison Med instead of Michigan City! There's really no comparison.

I had one of my advisers (Diane Lefer) at Vermont College when I was getting my MFA ask me what I thought about a famous author (whom I won't name) who writes a lot of his fiction about criminals and the joint. I told her that while I enjoyed his fiction, I didn't buy a word of it. His stuff sounded like it came from a guy who'd spent a night or two in the drunk tank or maybe spent a few hours as a reporter in a joint. There's no way such experiences count for anything at all. It's like those kids who go through the "Scared Straight" programs. They may go inside the walls and they may even have inmates pretending to "break bad" on them, but it's not even close to a real experience. These kids know they're not going to wake up in the morning without watching their backs every second for the next several years. There's only one way to get that experience and that's to get sentenced and actually live it.

The "Scared Straight" shows are really a joke. I've watched a bunch of them and to begin with, the kids are surrounded by hacks who, if an inmate actually broke bad with them, would have the guy in the hole and the kid hustled out immediately. It's a stretch to think these kids actually get scared, especially since some of them have already done juvie time and may have already had somebody try to get their brown eye. And, they never have truly bad dudes participating in these shows—most look like the kind of guys who the *real* bad dudes are breaking bad on. There's no way the prison is going to let these kids hang out with Charlie Manson or his cellmate, Roger Smith, the "most-stabbed inmate in history." The guys who participate in this program are trying to get out by doing this kind of "community service," and have a boatload of good time to even qualify for the program. It's a good idea in conception, maybe, but I'd be surprised if any other than the truly naïve are much influenced by the experience.

Anyway, in *Just Like That*, the reader will get a bit truer look at the joint than they will in most books…There's a scene where Jake (the protagonist) and Bud are in a swamp in Louisiana and just shooting the shit about fears; this scene shows the criminal mind fairly accurately. Cathy Johns, then the assistant warden at the Louisiana prison at Angola (the Farm), read this and wrote me that it was "the truest account of the criminal mind" that she'd ever read. Should be. I was a criminal for a long time.

Hope you enjoy it!

Blue skies,
—Les

(*) "Popcorners" is a term an old girlfriend of mine gave to retirees. One time, we were at an American Legion drinking and they were having a dance with one of those big balls swirling overhead, and we looked in at the dance, and she said the dancers looked like "popcorn popping" with their white hair bobbing up and down. Ergo…"popcorners."

ONE

We were having beans this meal. That's not news—when we *don't* have beans, that's news. My main concern was not biting down on a rock. There are rocks all the time in the beans. If I looked around, I would see everyone else eating the way I was. Carefully, so as not to bite down on a rock. As if I cared.

There are long rows of inmates, just shy of five hundred of us at a sitting when we eat. Twenty to a table, ten on each side. Five rows of tables, five tables to a row. There are no tablecloths on the tables, just the metal painted gray, gloss finish. They feed us in shifts. We do almost everything in shifts. They don't want us all together. That could lead to trouble.

Rows of blue denim. Guys in blue denim eating at gray tables. Civil War motif in 1968. Boy, wasn't that the truth!

Not every table is full. Here and there is an empty seat. Individuals who didn't feel like beans tonight or stayed in their cell for another reason. I see a few spots where there are two vacant seats right next to each other and I can guess why they skipped supper. There are more absent than usual but that's because it's payday—when the state issues you your monthly chit—and everybody has been to the commissary buying bags of cookies and Pall Malls because of their length—more for the money. If I hadn't owed all my money out, I'd be back in the cell myself, eating Oreos and not worrying about busting a tooth.

The man across from me said, "Hey, look at that." He kicked me under the table.

I looked where he was looking and saw one of the inmate cooks walking fast with a meat cleaver in his hand, held down, blade up. He was walking like a man with a mission, in a straight line. He walked with even, precise steps, each stride the same length as the previous and the same speed. Not slow, not fast, just the same. He walked in a line that could have been marked off with a carpenter's plumb line chalked on the concrete, up to the head table, and his last three steps were like this: The hand with the cleaver went back on one like a pendulum, swung forward in an underhand arc on two, and sank into this inmate's blue denim belly on three. It was as smooth a thing as I had ever seen. The man whose belly received the cleaver had cooperated as if they had practiced their little dance together for hours. He stiffened in awareness on the first of those last three steps, began to rise on the second and was fully upright on the third, in perfect position.

There was a general hubbub of noise like what you'd expect. I forgot to check the spoonful of beans I just put in my mouth and bit down hard on a pebble. I was almost done with the meal and I did that. Stupido!

They were locking us down. I went in first, when we were all in front of our cells. What was the point in staying out on the tier walk for just a few extra seconds? We were going to be in all night anyway.

My cellmate was awake, a guy named Larry something, I kept forgetting his last name. The last month before your parole hearing they put you in a cell, keep you from some of the trouble in the dorms. Larry was all right but he wasn't

Dusty. Bud had already been cut loose back in November. I missed my friends from K-Dorm.

He was holding a magazine and pretending to read it. I knew why he had skipped supper. He didn't like waiting until I went to sleep to masturbate. "Look," I'd said, plenty of times. "Go ahead and stroke the bald man. It's none of my business. Just don't get any ideas." But, he was from a small town. I guess that's the reason. Shy, you see?

"What happened at the chow hall?"

"What? Oh…I don't know. Somebody got whacked."

"I heard. Franklin told me." Franklin was the hack downstairs, put us in for the night. He would sit down at the desk all night and read those True Police Story magazines, pick his teeth with a folded-up gum wrapper. You could see him wince when the aluminum hit a filling. You'd think he'd learn, get a regular toothpick, discover floss string.

"Franklin said it was a guy from K-Dorm. He said Susie did it."

He was right. It was Susie. I could see that, the part I happened to pay attention to.

He went on, "Susie! That guy's a mountain! One big sissy!"

"Doesn't matter how big you are, you got a meat cleaver, you're the biggest guy around, regardless your size."

"Yeah." He laughed. "Franklin said the guy ran out the chow hall with the cleaver sticking out of his stomach. He said he was holding it in with his hands."

I didn't say anything. What could I add to that?

"He said he ran all the way across the grinder to the hospital. He said he got halfway up the steps before he died. He said he fell halfway up the steps and all his guts just popped out. God!"

I had the idea I was supposed to say something, but what?

"Is that what happened? Where were you?"

I saw what he wanted. He wanted details. Franklin must not have seen it himself. Well, of course not. He was over here in J Block. One of the other hacks must have come by, filled him in. They'd kept us over at the chow hall a half-hour longer, brought in some extra guards, blew the big steam whistle makes all the guards shit 'n git, all that stuff. They didn't want trouble. A thing like that…

"I guess that's about right. I didn't see that but it sounds about right."

"Didn't you see it? Goddamn Jake., you were right there! What happened?"

I looked at him.

"I don't know. I guess that's what happened. I wasn't paying attention. It was just some grudge thing. I bit a rock."

"A rock?"

"Yes. In the beans. I guess I'll have to go to the dentist tomorrow. I'm not too thrilled about that."

He just shook his head and picked up his magazine. He turned over, his back to me and began turning the pages. I could tell he was disgusted that I hadn't had any juicy details. He turned the pages faster and faster, making a lot of noise.

My tooth was starting to really hurt now. I could feel pieces of filling or maybe the tooth itself. That rock had done a job, probably cracked the actual enamel. I got up and went over and tried to look inside my mouth in the mirror, but the mirror was metal, not glass, and it's hard to see something like that in a metal finish. After a while, I gave it up and went back and climbed up on my bunk. I tried to think about other things, keep my mind off my tooth. It was throbbing at a pretty good clip now. I wondered if I yelled down to Franklin, would he get me an aspirin.

In a little while, I began to doze off. Almost.

"Jake."

I said, "Huh?"

"You got three weeks, huh?"

He was talking about my parole hearing.

"That's right."

"You'll be back, Jake. I can guarantee it."

Everybody always says that. It's jealousy, that's all it is.

"You remember Melrose, Jake.?"

Melrose was a little skinny black guy in the cell next to me, a long time ago, after getting out of quarantine, when I first came to the Pendleton Reformatory. He was slowwalking somebody for a carton of butts and the guy came by and threw acid in his face. He lay in his cell and screamed all night. The hack downstairs just kept on reading his magazine. It wasn't Franklin; it was somebody else, but he read the same kinds of magazines, True Crime, stuff like that. Hacks all seemed to share the same literary tastes. In the morning, after we went out for chow, they came and got Melrose, who was down to a little occasional whimper by then. None of us heard anything, we said, when they asked. When Melrose got out of the hospital, he had pink blotches all over his face, looked like bubble gum. Permanent blotches. Also, he lost an eye. That happened on my very first night in the population, before I learned to shut crap like that out, become invisible.

"You cried when that happened to Melrose. I heard you. I was above you, top tier. You just got assigned to J Block. I knew who you were, new guy all the niggers wanted to fuck."

"I was new. It was a shock. I was probably scared. So what?"

"You yelled at the guard. I told you to shut up, you'd get us all in trouble."

Damn, that tooth was acting up!

"So what?"

"So what is a guy gets whacked now and you don't even

care. You got a problem, Jake."

My tooth really began to throb. I swung my feet over the edge, leaned over and grabbed the bars and brought my face up to them.

"Hey! Franklin! I need an aspirin! Up here in twenty-two. Jake Mayes, four-nine-oh-two-eight."

"Your heart is hard, man. Ask me, you're institutionalized," Larry said, still on the same subject. Like I asked him or something.

For some reason I thought of my dad. I wished there was some way he could've been a fly on the wall, seen how I handled this. He thought he was some kind of serious hard case. Maybe I'd write him a letter, kind of casually mention what had happened, act like I was more concerned with what we were having for dessert than seeing this guy get whacked. What the hell—I was getting out pretty soon. I'd bring it up in a conversation some time, like something that had slipped my mind it was so unimportant.

An image of Susie burying the cleaver in that guy came up in my mind, and I couldn't remember what the other guy looked like, who he was, even though I vaguely remembered seeing him around the yard. I could feel that tooth though. It was throbbing like nobody's business. I couldn't keep my tongue off of it. You know how it is when you got a tooth hurting like that. You can't keep your tongue away from it. You have to keep worrying it. That's what I did. I kept worrying that tooth.

TWO

I made parole and I'd been on the bricks seven months.

One minute I was on my way to work and the next minute I wasn't.

Bang.

Just like that.

I did stuff like that all the time. I'd be talking to a guy, a friend even, and the idea would overtake me to sucker-punch him. For no reason. I just knew it would feel good. Or, I'd pull up to a 7-Eleven for cigarettes and get inside, and all the way to the counter, money out and everything, nothing on my mind except get some smokes, and something would click, maybe the way the clerk kept reading his Playboy instead of waiting on me right away, and before I knew it, I had my piece out and the guy, the clerk, is on the floor, and I'm hightailing it to the car with a bagful of cash. Bang. Just like that. Don't ask me why these things happened like they did. I don't have a clue. They just did.

"Bud," I said, into the receiver. "I'm a block away, at the QuikStop and I'm leaving town. How about it? You tired of Fort Wayne pussy?"

Bud and I go way back, even before Pendleton, although that's where we hooked up and became serious rappies. I was cellmates with his friend Dusty and then when we got into K-Dorm, Bud was already there, and it became us three. The Three Musketeers, all for one and one for all. Bud protected me since he was the biggest, and we both looked out for Dusty, who was too sweet looking for any judge to have ever sentenced.

Dusty had the worst rap sheet. He'd killed a gas station attendant when he was sixteen because the guy wouldn't let him have any gas—said he was closing and the pumps were locked up. I heard the story a million times.

What started it was Dusty'd stole this car and was two blocks from home, some apartment where he was shacked up with a fourteen-year-old hooker, when the car ran out of gas.

"Pissed me off, he did," Dusty said in that voice of his that jumped registers practically every other word, so he waited until the guy got off and watched where he went. He had this old pickup parked out back a' the station, and this guy, he just went back there and sat on the driver's side and began nipping at a bottle he had there. "See?" Dusty said. "The guy wouldn't take ten minutes to sell me a buck's worth of gas, and it wasn't like he had to *be* someplace." That's when he really got pissed, Dusty said. Went and fetched the jack handle from his trunk and snuck around and clopped him through the window, busted the glass and his head, same time. He hit him a couple more licks, just to get the mad out.

After that, according to Dusty, he just walked on home. He had bad luck though. The cops followed his tracks in the snow right up to the apartment where he was and came in, no warrant, nothing—that was what Dusty said—and there he was, buck-naked in bed with this fourteen-year-old, the gas station guy's blood all over his shirt, which was laying on the floor. His girlfriend was slurping the Big Gulp and just about bit it off when that door came flying open, he said. We all got a picture of that and snorted.

He did the first part of his stretch at the Indiana Boys' School—account of his age—but he didn't last there long, after he killed another boy, stabbed him with a straightened-out laundry pin, and they had no choice but to send him over to Pendleton, which is where we met when they put him in my cell.

Young, sweet-looking thing, but a stone-cold killer. Like that mattered, where we were. Throw a rock any direction, hit about ten-eleven stone-cold killers on a lazy Tuesday morning. He was bad but not so bad for there. He was eighteen when I moved into his cell, and had twelve more years to go before they transferred him to Michigan City. That's the way they did it then, back in the sixties and early seventies. Under thirty you went to Pendleton and over thirty to Michigan City. Young cons over here, old cons over there. It's all changed now, boot camps, youth camps, shit like that all over the place. Candy-ass places for all the little suburban punks got caught trying to supplement their allowances selling dope to other punks. Pussy for real cons.

Anyway, that's how I ran into Bud again; he was in the cell next to us and was from South Bend, same as me, and we just hit it off. It was on the straight, too. Lots of folks think everybody in the joint is either a sissy or a daddy, but there are lots of friendships that are neither, just guys who get along same as on the bricks, and that's the way it was for all three of us.

That's why I called Bud. When I got out, even though I was from South Bend, I took the bus to Fort Wayne, where Bud had gone himself instead of back to South Bend. You know, escape the "influences." Bud, he had got me a job through PACE, the do-good outfit, businessmen who want to help ex-convicts, and the job was in Fort Wayne with Bud, who got cut loose seven months before me. In fact, the job was at the same barber shop he worked at. Most of the other guys were ex-cons, too. The owner was himself an ex-con. Good guy, but a boozer. We used to have to go in and roust him off the stool when he had a customer. Sat in there hitting one of his hidden bottles. Vodka, so the customers couldn't smell anything. That's what he thought, anyway. Most of his customers were drunker than he was, usually, pals of his from down at the North Star Bar and Tap. Once in a while, some mother, didn't know him, came in with her kid. We'd bet, usually fives, how long it'd be before he'd clip the tyke's ear, the way he shook. See, a little boy's skin is soft, you can even cut it with the clippers when they're set on triple-ought. You got to have them bend way over when you cut the back. Stretches the skin so you don't cut it. There's also this little hollow in the middle of the neck that little boys have until they get older, and you have to bend the head over to flatten it out so you can cut the hair there. The boss, Wayne Ferguson, he'd forget to bend the kid's head over. Get to talkin' with his buds and nail the kid. One thing he liked to do was talk. Guy like that, in the joint, we call him a Jeff Chandler 'cause he's always jaffin. Selling you bullshit, a wolf ticket, is what he was always doing.

He used to tell the mother that the kid only cried because *she* was there and somehow he'd convince her to leave while he finished. You could see the tears start to well up in her eyes as she went out into the other room, leaving her crying baby behind. Soon's she'd leave, he'd grab the kid's ear on that little hangy-downy part with his thumb and finger and squeeze hard. He'd get down real low, to the kid's level, and he'd say; *Now, you little sumbitch. You let out a peep, I'm gonna rip your ear off.*

It was a wonder ol' Wayne never got arrested. Either the kid's mother didn't believe her kid when she got home, or else she figured, what's the use. One thing, he didn't have much repeat business in kids.

That was another thing. Me, Bud and Dusty all got into the prison barber school. Coming out into the population from quarantine, I'd started out in I.D., Identification, where we take your mug shot and print up your rap sheet. It was a good lick but I could see the handwriting on the wall; this was a job that was so good you had to keep paying somebody the whole time or color your ass gone, and gone meant you had to go over to the laundry or the mess hall to work. Unh-uh. Be one of three honkys in the middle of fifty brothers got tear drops tattooed on their cheeks?

"Barber school," Dusty said. "I got a hack likes me, Mr. Jones. He got me in, he can do it for you, too. I'll set it up. You got to act like I say when you talk to him."

So I applied for barber training and sure enough, I'm in there, cutting flattops on the white guys and "lines" on the brothers; me, that never in a million years woulda figured I'd end up in that line of work. Lot of the white guys, they hated cutting lines on the bros, but me, I kinda enjoyed it. Only time I could hold a razor on a nigger and they couldn't do a thing about it. I used to talk to 'em, whisper shit in their ears. It's a wonder any of them came back—only they had no choice. The inmate played receptionist told them whose chair to sit in. I got a rep that way. Brothers would whisper, that's a crazy honky there, meaning me, and how they was going to get me sometime. They never did though. They knew if they tried and fucked up, sooner or later they'd have to sit in my chair and I had that razor.

At first I worried some about what my dad would think. He was what you'd think of as a real "man's man" and I was already in barber school three months before I said anything in my letters. I guess I thought he'd call what I was doing a "sissy" job, having my fingers in other people's hair, but I thought it over real good and ended up telling him. It wasn't like I was a *beautician*, and even if I was, so what? That's what I told him in my letter and what I also said was that I couldn't get into the body shop where they fixed the cars of the hacks and various instructors. That was a lie, of course. I hadn't even considered the body shop. He never wrote back, which was normal; he never wrote anyway, so I don't know if he approved but fuck it, who cares, anyway? It's my life is the way I figured it and if he didn't like it, fuck'm. I'd like to see how he'd handle it in here himself, Mr. Tough Ass, like he always thought he was. I tried not to think about what Dad thought but it wasn't always that easy. Besides I was twenty-three. Who gives a rat's ass what his "daddy" thinks, anyway!

Bud came over later when he saw how good a lick the school was, and then we all put in for K-Dorm, and that's how I spent most of my three years in the joint, barber school and K-Dorm, Bud, Dusty and yours truly. Our chairs were even side by side at the barber school—Bud in the middle, Dusty on the left and me on the right.

We played a lot of cards in K, mostly double-hand pinochle for cigarettes, candy bars. Blow jobs. "You lose this hand, you got to bend over." Shit like that. Me, Bud and Dusty, we never got into them kind of stakes but there were plenty who did. We played mostly for Oreos, Camels, green when we had it. Green is jailhouse slang for real money, bills. Bills were contraband but there was plenty floating around.

Barbering was a pretty good lick, and for something never crossed my mind I'd ever do, I found out I was pretty good at it. There's something about a sharp-as-your-ass Andis clipper blade biting into the back of somebody's neck hair, you starting to make a creation with just a few simple tools and your fingers, that's—*satisfying.*

"Let me call my old lady," Bud said, not even asking where I was, which was the QuickStop, or where I was going, which I didn't know, or why—none of the kinds of questions a straight john would of asked. Just, "Let me call Kimmie. She's working down at Parkview Hospital in housekeeping. Give me an hour to pack."

To kill time, I invested in a call to my brother. "Thirty-five cents," the operator said. "For three minutes."

"Shit," I said. "I just want to use this for a minute, lady, not buy it," but I was talking to a ring tone. Bitch.

"Hello," I said. "Is Raymond there?" It was my sister-in-law, Ruthy Ann. I figured it was a Tuesday, Ray might've had a hangover and skipped work. I had his work number if I needed it, but it turned out I'd called the right number first.

"—fuck you calling this early for?" he said. "I'm still in bed."

"Yes," I said.

A woman with a little blonde boy, about four maybe, pushed by me to get to the cooler where the pop was, and I had to hug the wall to let them by. He was crying he wanted a Coke-Cola and she was saying it was too early for pop; he should have a fruit juice, how about orange or maybe cranberry? The cranberry was on sale, she was explaining to this little brat: I could get two, one for you and one for me, honey. I waited till they were past to resume my own conversation.

"Jake? You still there? You calling from jail?"

Raymond calmed down when it became clear I wasn't after bail money, was *offering* him something instead.

"I got a bunch of clothes, two nice leather jackets, both full-length, and other stuff, records. There's about an eighth in a bag in one of the pockets of the brown one."

"And I can have it all?" he said, waiting for the catch. "You owe rent or something doncha? Will the landlord let me in? You still in that place in Ft. Wayne, off Lake?"

I laughed. "Yeah, and I'm paid up for two more weeks, Ray. I'll call him, tell him to let you in. I'll even see if he'll give you the two weeks I already paid. I doubt it though. There's some deposit money, too, but I think he's gonna want that to fix the door."

"Well say, it's worth a try," he said. "Maybe I'll just *use* it for two weeks. Have some poker parties." I could see his mind working, figuring out how to capitalize on his sudden good fortune, only I figured it wasn't poker he had in mind. I wondered if Ruthy Ann was standing there listening, and did he think she was that dumb. He was going to drive all the way down from South Bend to Fort Wayne for *poker parties*? Sure. "Where you going, Jake? You told Mom? What'd she say?"

"No," I said to the second question, and "I don't know, Ray; I can't say for sure," to the first.

"Hey, Jake."

"What?"

"How come you weren't at Dad's funeral?"

"I was."

"Fuck you were. I didn't see you. You wearing your Captain Midnight Invisible Shield?"

"Maybe. Fuck you, Ray. I was there. Don't worry about it. I just didn't go in the church is all. I paid my respects in private."

"Yeah."

"Yeah."

When I hung up, the kid's mother had gone to the front by the cigarettes and Slim Jims and the kid was opening and slamming shut the cooler door. I guess she'd given up on him. Me, I'da left him. Climbed in my car when he wasn't looking and went out and took in a movie, hope he got run over by a beer truck, something.

"Kid," I said, crooking my finger at him and bending over. "Kid, you get the cranberry juice like your momma told you. I got a gun in here and if you don't I'm going to shoot you in the leg." He stood there a minute and I was half out the door when he came screaming up to his mom. I looked back in the car and seen her, and she had the little shit up in her arms glaring at me. So were some other people. Fuck'm, is what I thought. I was in a mood.

I started to pull out then changed my mind. One of those things that were always happening, don't ask me why. I went back in.

"Line up by the coolers," I said, waving my hog. "Fill it," I said to the clerk, this kid who was a poster for the pimple-cure industry, shoving one of the plastic bags on the counter at him.

While the clerk was putting the money in the bag, I told the little kid's mother, "Honey, you go back and get you a can of that cranberry juice." The smart thing would have been to get the hell out of there, but I wasn't done.

"Drink it," I told the kid. He only started bawling. "Drink it or I'm gonna blow out your kneecap, you little shithead." His mama seen I was serious, slapped the living shit out of her kid, held the can for him while he tried to choke some down, both of them boohooing. It mostly got all over the front of his shirt, way he was moving around, looked like blood.

"You mind your mama, son," I said, going out the door. "Less you want to end up like me."

I headed over to Bud's place. On the way I dumped out the bag on the seat and tried to count it. No more than fifty-sixty bucks it looked like, mostly ones and a few fives. One lousy ten.

Me and Bud go back a long way. Back to my first day in the joint. Even farther back than that. On the street when I was robbing and pillaging the straights I'd run into him sometimes. Once, about three in the morning, at the Kozy Korner Koffee Shop, the outlaw hangout in South Bend, a couple of my rap partners and me were hanging out in a back booth, cracking on a couple of prosties in the booth next to us, and I saw Bud talking to some babe at the counter. I'd seen him around, only I didn't know who he was, then.

All of a sudden she cracks him with a closed fist, a big ol' strawberry popping up where she hit him on the cheek. Well, Bud doesn't say a word, only grabs her arm and hauls her out the back door, her cussing and trying to kick him. Naturally, we all pile out of the joint to see what he'd do. All he did was smack her once, open hand, and then she goes into her purse, quick, like these greasers will do, and comes out with this little pocket knife, which she sticks in his neck, clear down to the handle. It's stuck there like some dart lost its way during a bar game, and he reaches up and plucks it out like it's a mosquito just stung him. And laughs. Blood's running down his neck, tie-dying his white T-shirt, and he just laughs.

The way he laughs freeze-dries her—you could just see that—just nails her to the spot; her face turns as white as first-date panties—even in the dark we could all see that— and she just turns and runs while he stands there grinning. Chilly.

Tough mother.

After that I made his acquaintance, talked to him once in a while. We got to be friends.

He had this old Studebaker Lark he fixed up so he could remove the steering wheel and steer with a control stick between his knees. His brothers helped him engineer the car in the body shop they owned with their dad.

We'd get some unsuspecting dude in the car on the pretext of cruising and slamming down some cans of Drewry's Mountie Piss, and after we'd killed a six-pack or two, head out west on Lincolnway, out toward the airport where the houses thin out and the cornfields start. When we reached the country, right before the airport, Bud would get the Lark up to about eighty-five, which was top end. They shoulda named that car the Cocker Spaniel, it was such a pooch. Hell, the real lark, the bird, could outfly it with one wing broke. We always let the new guy sit in the front with Bud, and I'd sit in the back. We'd roll down all the windows for effect, have the wind screaming in, and Bud would start weaving back and forth, criss-crossing the center line. He'd say he was dizzy, felt like passing out. All of a sudden, he'd pluck the wheel loose and hand it to the guy saying, "Oh man, I'm going out. It's all black. Here—*you* drive." He'd punch the gas pedal down all the way as he slumped forward.

I parked the car about a block from Bud's apartment and smoked four or five cigarettes. Different people strolled by, giving me the once-over, so I decided to go ahead and pick him up, ready or not. Turns out he'd been waiting for me.

THREE

We were clear the other side of Anderson on 69 before Bud even mentions anything about where we're going. We're about ten minutes from the 465 bypass around Indianapolis when he said, "South, huh?"

I grinned and squeezed between my legs the can of Miller's Genuine Draft he'd handed me so's I could pop the top. We had all the windows down, front and back, and were cruising at seventy, every so often rolling them up when we went past a pig farm, until we got drunk enough we didn't care. That stretch of 69 you could do sixty-five, legal, and they always gave you an extra ten. "That okay?"

We were listening to the Inkspots, the only tape I had. I was driving Bud nuts, listening to "If I Didn't Care" over and over.

"Fuck an A," he said, popping his own, beer mist spraying all over, goobering up the window. "Next time though, we get Stroh's. Can we listen to the rest of that tape? You got anything else? That fucking song's fucking depressing, Jack. We're going south, let's get us some country tunes. Willie Nelson."

"Stroh's isn't beer, Bud. It's wino piss. They hire derelicts from Milwaukee at the brewery t'pee in the vats, then they sell it to farmers like you that don't know good beer. Nobody drinks beer can drink that crap. They find out you like

Stroh's at a good bar, they start serving you Shirley Temples, water back."

This was like old times.

We drank all the way down, listening to the Spots and a Waylon Jennings tape Bud picked up at a truck stop outside of Evansville just before we crossed the bridge.

This trip was my idea and I didn't have a clue where we were going. *Warm* was all I cared about.

Together we anted up the pot, and we had four hundred and twelve bucks and some silver between us. Three-fifty of that was mine, counting what I'd got from the QuickStop. I didn't tell Bud about that. No sense in worrying him for no reason. I hadn't bothered to go back to my apartment to get my clothes and things, but I wasn't totally a moron, either. I'd stopped by the bank on the way to Bud's place and closed out my bank account.

"If I'd known the bitch'd cleaned me out, I wouldn't have called her and told her I was leaving," he said, soon as he climbed in the car. "I got sixty bucks total, home-boy. If I'd known she went through my pants last night, I woulda went over to the hospital, made some excuse and jacked her up for some. I fucked up, calling her first."

It didn't matter. We figured to go as long as our money lasted and find something wherever that was, a job or something, or if we happened on a place we liked before we were broke, we'd do the same there. Neither of us gave it much thought. We were both thieves, at least that's what we'd both done time for, although each of us had done a few other things, too. Armed robbery, strong-arm robbery, dope, things like that, the usual, guys like us. Though that wasn't the only thing Bud got popped for. He got busted for rape with the other stuff, but that's another story.

I had my Mossberg twelve gauge and a twenty-two rifle in the trunk and Bud had brought a Police Special .38 with the numbers filed off, which I made him hide in the wheel well in the trunk, case we got stopped. Under the spare, which was flat. I put my .45 there, too. It wasn't that we were planning on doing a job, it was just that we both knew how to, and if worse came to worse, well, it wasn't the end of the line like it would be for some folks.

That night we kept an eye out for a cheap motel close to a bar and found one just across the line into Tennessee. I don't remember the name of the town, some little podunk where the bar and motel up on the highway seemed to *be* the town. Gobbler's Knob or something was probably the name of it, most of them one-horse towns was called something like that. Finger Fucker's Ferry, Joe-Bob's Dell. Weird names, you wondered where they came from, what the history was.

We checked into a double and it was a bit pricey seeing as how it looked like a pack of former slave quarters or something—bunch of little shacks all painted white at one time, peeling and gone to hell by now and practically falling down; but as I say, we were flush and said what the fuck. Twenty-eight bucks and three for the key, get it back when you turned the key in. First thing we checked was the air conditioning, and it worked fine though it was loud. Sounded like it was about to blow a gasket but the air was frosty and kicked out in buckets. The sheets were clean, too. There was a few roaches but not the big ones you see in Florida. These were hardly nothing, little bitty things. There was a Bible and a phone book that was smaller than my rap sheet.

This was one of those rent-it-by-the-hour dumps, couples coming and going all hours and mostly drunk or high whole time we were there, and I figure we copped the only double in the bunch, musta used it for the big orgies. Big ol' hillbilly Cadillacs parked all over; '57 two-door Chevies with California rakes, painted either black or red. Only two colors they could use and still be in the hillbilly race-driver club probably. Once in a while a '56 Ford would pull in, most likely the maverick hillbilly. Seemed like every time we turned around that night somebody was spraying our door with gravel, trying to impress their little girlfriends, but hell, we all done that shit, even up north.

Well, we have found the action place we said to each other and jumped in and took turns showering and loading up with the aftershave, turned out in our best threads—me in my truck stop rodeo shirt—and then heading over across the highway for the bar, which was knee-deep in big-titted gals and guys with beards and cowboy hats. I bet we were the only guys without chin hair. Must have been a local thing, and it sure made us stand out. Which was good and bad. Good 'cause the women noticed we was fresh meat and bad 'cause the local bad asses noticed we was fresh meat, too.

The joint was called the Blue Pony—where they got *that* from god only knows—only it was full of blue neon lights and signs. No ponies though, flamingos that looked more like blue turkeys, cartoon characters, and dogs or something I guess were supposed to be dogs. And every beer sign in the world, most of them red. They shoulda called it "Neon City" 'stead of the pony thing. Who knows what goes through a cracker's head?

We didn't have to wait long. Just got our first beers and cracked wise at the waitress, this peroxide burnout couldn't been much more than sixteen, when these two Hill Williams—that's what Bud liked to call them—sidled up and sat down at our table, uninvited, a big, mean-looking doofus with a scar alongside his chin looked like wasn't put there with no Gillette Blue Blade, and his sidekick, a little wormy kind of character with a Snidely Whiplash pencil 'stash and a goatee with a vitamin deficiency, kept him from growing the complete, filled-out article.

"You boys are new in town," said the moose. I swear to

God, that's what he said, and it was all either of us could do to keep from busting out laughing. I peeped at Bud and he at me, and I knew he was having the same trouble I was, keeping the snickers down or keeping from asking the guy if maybe he'd seen too many John Wayne movies. Before anything else happened, Bud stuck his hand over the big guy's mitt that was on the table, and the guy's hand just disappeared. Just fucking disappeared. I told you, Bud was a big guy. Six-six and about that wide.

Then it got interesting.

Bud leaned over and put his face right up in the guy's mug, up under his Stetson, and said, real soft, "I just want to tell you straight off, Large Rufus, or whatever they call you hereabouts. Once I got my leg broke when some clumsy ox like you fell on it after I stroked him. Now I ain't too crazy about that happening again, I've got to tell you. The way I see it, that could happen again, so I made my mind up a long time ago, I wasn't going to be laid up in some bed six weeks with a cast on, scratchin' dead skin with a coat hanger. No sir, I ain't gonna let that happen again or even the remote chance of it."

I was watching Bud's hand turn white as he began to squeeze the other guy's and at first the guy tried to get his hand loose, kind of casual-like, like he wasn't really trying at all, only had an itch he needed to scratch, but Bud had him in a killer grip. I swear I heard a bone pop but I can't verify that. I do know sweat was jumping out on the guy's forehead, and it wasn't a grin he had on his kisser. And this was a big guy himself, only he wasn't quite as big as Bud. This was a brown bear facing up to a grizzly. Why he didn't just reach over and thump Bud, I don't know. Well, yes, I do. I think the guy was smart underneath, 'spite of his pecker-wood looks.

Bud was going on in this low voice only us four could

hear, and his eyes was like little black shiny marbles, and he had this guy's *attention.*

"I just want to make this point, my friend. My buddy and me are just here for a little drink or two, and maybe if we get lucky we find some friendly girls. We're passin' through, be gone in the morning. We ain't after *your* girls, so if you want to point out which's yours, well, we'll lay offa them maybe. But if it's some trouble you want, then it's trouble you got, only this ain't gonna be no brawl like you been in before." He leaned in even closer, his nose not an inch from the other man's, and he said, "You need to know I'm a dumber hillbilly than you are, friend. I don't know when to quit. I'm truly afraid that once I start in on you, I won't stop till you're a dead motherfucker. In fact, I can practically guarantee I won't quit then. That would be a shame, Clyde, 'cause I can see you still got a lotta transmissions left to get to and repair in your lifetime, and there's gonna be a lot of sad motherfuckers with sick trannies at your funeral who're not gonna think too well of this. I got to tell you, be fair about it, this ain't gonna be your normal fair fight, Country. I like the eyes, is what I like, and while you're punching around in that silly way like I bet you're used to on account of you seen too many Clint Eastwood flicks, me, I like to get in close, use my digitals and go for the eyes. I get 'em, I eat 'em. Like grapes. But first I do *this* just so's I know which hand to watch for."

He put the mojo to it, squeezing the guy's hand and this time there was no mistake—something broke, a finger or a thumb. We all heard it crunch. The big guy had sand, some, anyway, as he didn't yell or nothing, but Lord! the sweat was coming off him in sheets, making him blink as fast as he could, and his color was white as a Ku Kluxer's dress robe. The other guy, I couldn't tell, but I bet myself he was putting a puddle under his chair or about to.

Bud took his hand away then, but first he patted the other

man's crippled-up paw, laying there like some mangled pup got caught in the combine. There was a little white thing sticking out, mighta been a bone, where the skin had broke, and some blood, just a trickle. He patted it gently, and the man winced and drew it away, holding it in his other hand like it was some wounded bird he'd found along the road. He sat there a minute staring at Bud—in fact, he hadn't taken his eyes from Bud's—and then he looked away, down, and got up, turned, and walked to the front door and out, holding his hand the whole time. The other clown sat there a minute as if confused, had found himself in the wrong place by accident, maybe, and then he stood himself up and went out the front door a little faster than his sidekick had.

"You're an amazement," I said to Bud, a grin breaking across my face, and I started to say something else on the same subject when he held up a finger.

"Hold up, home-boy," he said. "We're not out of the woods yet. Get the shit-eatin' grin off your face."

I realized what he was saying. Hell, I should have known better from my time in the joint. Never front a guy, make him lose face in public. In this case, even though Jim-Bob and Little Ernie had departed, us laughing about the little confrontation would be like laughing at all the others—that's *family*, places like that, and there were too many for us, bad as we might be. Well, bad as *Bud* might be, although I wasn't exactly no slouch at bustin' heads, either. It came right down to it I seen he was right and I wiped the smile off my kisser.

He read the hand right. The locals left us alone and the tension settled down and we had us a few beers, checking out the talent. There was some uglos but there was some good ones, too, some that smiled back, gave us a look.

Along about the third or fourth round he finally got around to it.

"It's your girlfriend isn't it? Why we're doing this, why

we're sitting here in cotton country instead of over at the North Star on State?"

I admitted it was. "Yeah. I got it pretty bad, Bud."

"Must be. You're still on parole aren't you?"

He knew I was.

"And you didn't even call in to quit your job did you, home-boy? I *know* you didn't get permission from your P.O. t'do this. Fuck, man," Bud said, shaking his head admiringly. "You're a gen-u-wine twenty-four carat fuckup. You're gonna be back there with Dusty, and who's gonna save your ass this time? Was it that Donna, that redhead I seen you with at the Three Rivers Festival? Big tits she's proud of?"

I cleared my throat, took a swig of beer, tried to look at him but couldn't quite make it.

"Yeah. I even tried to take the pipe, man. Some shit, huh?" I was embarrassed as soon as I said that. I don't know why I did, except we were like brothers and I figured if any-one could understand, Bud could.

"You're shittin' me."

"No." I thought again about the last few days. "I got me this room at Motel Six, you know, the one out on Coliseum Boulevard, out toward Harvester. By Azars. The one has the tittie bar behind it. Three days. Sat around in my skivvies with the TV off and the shades down. Didn't know if it was day or night most of the time. Didn't do nothin' but sit there and eat Jack Daniels and chocolate doughnuts. Did a bottle a day. Fuck, I don't do a bottle a *week*."

"So, how—"

I grinned, or tried to. "All I can say is I can't shave with my Norelco now. Fucking cord's busted. You got a razor I could borrow maybe?" I rubbed my neck. It was still sore. Then, I did laugh. "I paid a lot of money for that damn thing. You'd think the cord'd be stronger! Think the war-ranty's good on something like that?"

I looked at him and took a deep breath.

"I was gonna do it again, do it till I got it right, only I laid there awhile on the floor thinking that now I was gonna have to go out and buy something stronger, a rope, and I started to wonder what places were still open had rope for sale on a Sunday and then I wondered that if I was to find such a place would they take a check 'cause I only had a couple of bucks in cash left, and then I remembered I would have to go back to my apartment 'cause that's where my checkbook was—I could see it in my mind, sitting on the dresser, and then I thought—what the hell am I doing? If it is this much trouble then the hell with it! I would much rather spend my time doing something more fun that took less effort. So I did. I got up and turned on the TV. I didn't think about leaving town then—that's the honest to God truth. I did that this morning, driving over to Harvey's, but I might have started to think about it last night while I was lying there thinking about what a fuckup I was at killing myself, who knows? Anyway, here I am and here we are and what do you think of that? No, don't answer that. I just want to get drunk and see if we can get laid. I already forgot about what's-her-name."

"Donna."

"Yeah. Whatever." We both laughed.

"Pussy's pussy."

Yeah, there was that—Bud was right, but then again he was wrong. I'd always thought that, too—pussy was pussy— all cats look alike in the dark—all that shit—and mostly that's true, I guess, but Donna...well, Donna was...well, *different.* I can't think of a better word.

It was all kinds of things, me and Donna. The way she fucked. She screwed you like you and her were the last two motherfuckers on earth, and if she coulda got to pick who she was gonna get to play Adam and Eve with, it wouldn'ta been nobody else but you. That kind of shit.

She all the time was making you think. This is a good one. This is pure Donna. One time we're vegging out in bed, Sunday morning, the papers spread all over the bed and us, and out of nowhere she says, "You ever notice that all the people who park in handicapped spaces drive Cadillacs?" I mean, who *thinks* of that kind of shit? Not me.

"Yeah," I said, coming back. "Being handicapped must pay good."

Then she said something else, added to what we started, and we had this whole conversation going—*funny*-ass shit. Half an hour we go on. Talking with her was like talking to another guy, a brother or something. She never needed any of that bullshit fake-ass crap most girls seem to crave, have to always be telling them their eyes were like diamonds, shit like that. We lay there, rapping like a couple of buds and it was even better because you sure can't roll your buddy over and take one. Not me, anyway. It was like having a pard, only ten times better because you had the sex, too, and the sex was only the best I ever had. But that was Donna. She had this other side, too, not so good.

"Why'd you break up with her?"

Because of my dad, I thought, but I didn't tell Bud that. I didn't want to bring up the funeral, even think about it. I didn't tell him about her stabbing Patsy, either, or about the baby she aborted.

"I don't know. Lots of reasons."

That was it. We didn't talk any more about it. I didn't want to now that it was out, and Bud didn't bring it up again. About an hour later we hooked up with some honeys, couple of dishwater blondes, and walked 'em back over to the motel, along with a bottle and some ice we got from the bartender, and had us some fun with the girls, only Bud caught the clap from his, as we found out four days later when he took a very loud piss. My equipment worked just fine, thank you, and that made me feel a whole lot better about the future. The whole time we was doing the end-to-end buffet I thought about Donna only once or twice.

Funny. What I *did* think about was my dad. That was all the time happening—out of nowhere, for no reason, I'd be thinking about my father and wishing he was there, see me in action. See what a cocksman his number-one boy was. That was just nuts, the way that always happened, thinking about my pappy, me a grown man and all. I wonder if other guys think about their fathers when they're pulling a job, a robbery, or going down on some gal. Right. I'm the idiot has the father ghost always popping up at the dumbest times. I wonder what the shrink back at Pendleton would think of that.

Don't even say it.

FOUR

That wasn't the end of it with those good ol' boys we'd run into earlier back at the Blue Pony. I shoulda known better. About an hour after we put the girls out, said our goodbyes, I just got my peepers quieted down when this soft *rap rap rap* came at the door.

Bud was snoring away, or at least putting a good show on to make it look like he was, so this looked like another job for Super Sucker, which would be me. At first I tried to ignore it, but the knocks got louder and I thought I heard a woman's voice. Being as the girls had been gone awhile and this was a vacation, meaning all the pussy I could get was one of the main goals, I padded over in my skivvies and opened the door a crack.

It was that bleached blonde from the bar. The one who waited on us.

"Yeah?" I said. "I bet you got a case of beer in your car and no opener. Come to borrow a church key from your friendly visiting Yankee? How close am I to a right guess?"

She giggled, which was the effect I was after. Lots of guys got the wrong idea about how to get in tight with the women. Most of them think it's got something to do with looks or money or some horseshit like that. I'm not saying those things don't help, but what really gets a woman to lay down with you is to tickle her funny bone. You hit that bone on her and she'll take care of the bone on you. That's why I was never without a wisecrack. Lots of prettier dudes than me didn't get half the poon I ended up with by accident. A woman who laughs feels generous and there's only one thing of value any of them got and they know it. That's the biggest secret there is on making it with the opposite sex. Look at the gals cracking up when the bars close and I'll lay any odds you want that the guy they go home with is the guy making 'em giggle. See, a guy who has the right kind of humor is going to be a fun guy in the hay. Why? Because he's confident and that's the trait they're really crazy for. A guy who hasn't got the right kind of attitude about himself is going to go around acting all kind of serious-like. Women sense this, just like they can also sense that a guy who's loosey-goosey and keeps 'em in stitches is one cocky, sure-of-himself son-uvabitch...and that's the guy they want to have over to their double-wides.

I don't think all this, except in kind of a short-hand way, when I see her standing outside our door, but I've been down this road so much I kind of already feel all this between us, and it doesn't take but a second for this knowledge to kick in and show in the way I act.

Mostly, that's a feeling you can take to the bank, brother, but this time I got to say I was wrong.

"I happened to see you boys come over here a while ago. Think I might come in?"

That was a question that only had one answer that fit.

"You come right on in, pretty lady," I said, swinging the door wide open.

Next thing I know, I'm lying flat on my back and the blonde's in my room...along with two guys who looked kinda familiar. I don't know which one was the one who kicked the door into my forehead and like to split it in two, but I'd bet even money it was the brown grizzly we'd been talking to earlier. Along with his little greasy partner.

The noise woke up Bud, only Bud wasn't much help. The big guy had a pistol in his hand and it was aimed right where it would really hurt if it went off accidentally. At Bud. I wasn't in any imminent danger, unless he took a forty-five degree tack.

"G'night, Ruby," the little one said. She gave me a shrug like she was almost sorry for setting me up and took a hike, shutting the door behind her.

Well. This was cozy. Just us four fun-lovin' young bucks in a motel room in Bumfuck, Tennessee, admiring Doofus's shiny gun. I don't mind admitting I was a little nervous. Bud, though; Bud was cool. Acted like this sort of stuff happened all the time.

"Hey, fellas," he said, swinging his long legs off the bed and rubbing sleep from his eyes like this was a couple of our poker-playing amigos come to roust us up for a game of draw poker.

"Get dressed, cowboy," the big one said. "We're going to take a ride."

"We've seen your fair city," Bud said, stretching back on the bed, folding his arms behind his head. "And I don't think we'd be all that interested in the tour you got in mind."

You could see this flustered the moose. I guess he was figuring on me and Bud acting like a couple of sissy-boy Yankees and rolling over for him. Truth is, if it had just been me, I'da probably had my clothes on already and been opening the door politely for these guys. You could see Paul Bunyan kind of getting it together in his little pea brain, trying to figure out what to do next, what with this unexpected hitch in his master plan—his eyebrows going down in that little mad V some folks get when they're upset. Before he could come up with a wrinkle on the plan Bud had just tweaked, Bud eliminated all that brain activity for him. He just kinda reached behind him under the pillow and brought out his own gun. I'd seen that gun before but I had no idea he'd brought it with him. It was a Smith & Wesson Police Special .38 he'd bought off some cop a long time ago in South Bend.

Mexican standoff.

The other guy reaches in his pocket and brings out a knife, a move I don't like all that much, as I don't happen to have a gun under my own pillow. Not that I didn't think I could take him. The guy looked like a true weenie, following around his big, ugly friend like he was bad his own self, when it was plain as the nose on Barbra Streisand he was not.

The moose started to open his mouth to say something when Bud just popped him.

Boom!

Fucking bullet started whizzing all over the place, skipping first off the guy's noggin and then the wall and then it ended up in the bathroom, smashing the mirror. Made one hell of a lot of racket for one little ol' slug.

When I peeked up over the side of the bed where I'd sort of thrown myself, I didn't see anybody but Bud, who was just lying there on his bunk, looking more pissed-off than anything.

Oh, fuck, I thought. We done killed some guy and the jury's gonna be all his cousins and brothers-in-law and the like. Our new cellmates were all going to be named Bubba and need extensive dental work. I'd just seen the movie *Deliverance* and I had a good idea what we were in for. I'd never done time in a southern prison, but if the movies I'd seen were halfway true to life, I'd take Pendleton any day. Better practice up on my squealing pig imitation.

Only the guy wasn't dead. Had blood all over him. All over him and half the room, but he wasn't dead. He started moaning and trying to sit up and Bud walked over and took the piece out of his hand, which he was still holding onto.

His partner just lay on the floor where he'd fallen—fainted, I think—and bawled like some woman just found out General Hospital'd been canceled.

"Here," Bud says and throws over a towel to the guy. "Your mascara's starting to run, sweetie." The guy picked it up and actually thanked Bud!

"It just bounced off his thick skull," Bud said to me. Now the big guy was down on his knees over the other guy, wiping the blood off his face. Sure enough, that's what it had done: Tore a neat little divot out of his temple, just in front of his ear, but that was it. It was weird how so much blood came out of such a little skid mark.

"What we gonna do with 'em?" I asked. I went over to Snidely, who was down to a few sniffles and some wide eyes by now, and took the knife from him. Polite little cuss. He not only handed it to me without my having to ask, but he turned it around and gave it to me handle first. I tiptoed over to the window and peeked out the curtain. "You suppose the cops are on the way?"

"Naw," Bud said. "We made more noise than that when we was banging these guys' girlfriends. Little ol' gunshot ain't gonna raise any eyebrows. They hear stuff like that all night." Which was true. Seemed like every half hour since we'd been there we'd heard either firecrackers or .22s popping, amongst the burning rubber left by cars smoking out of the parking lot. This was an active little town. "But, I do think it's time to move on. You never can tell when the local Smokey might decide to earn his pay and take a look. Especially when the car out front has plates that say 'Wander Indiana' on it."

Turns out Bud had a heck of a plan. Made both boys take off all their clothes—that was a look the little one gave me when Bud told them to do that! He musta seen *Deliverance*, too. That wasn't what Bud had in mind, though.

He wadded up all their clothes while I packed our gear and checked under the beds to be sure we weren't leaving anything. We weren't too worried about the motel owner identifying us, since we'd already taken the usual precaution of using somebody else's name on the register, along with a license number probably didn't exist. And this wasn't a big enough deal to go to the trouble of getting an artist's rendition out on the APB wires. Long as we could get out of the county, we'd be all right. Unless the big guy died, which didn't look too likely, as he was acting frisky and all kind of grumpy by now, telling us under his breath what he'd like to do to us if we'd just give him his gun back.

About five miles down the road, Bud pulled over and picked up their clothes from the back seat and flung them out into a field of some green stuff that looked like short corn on steroids. Right after them, he threw their car keys. Last thing to go sailing was both the guys' billfolds, but not until after he took out the cash, which wasn't much. Eleven dollars in the little guy's wallet and six in the other one. Bud kept the odd buck, saying since he was the genius who'd masterminded this robbery, he deserved the extra. It wasn't hardly worth arguing over, so I didn't.

All the way down the road we kept laughing until our cheeks hurt, imagining different scenarios the two naked guys back at the motel might be involved in. Especially since they couldn't just sneak out to their car and drive off. Not only had we taken their keys, but Bud had decided he needed a spare distributor cap and thought theirs might work on my car.

The good thing about all that business was that our fun with those boys, plus the earlier fun with the girls, had pretty much taken my mind off Donna.

For a while, anyway.

FIVE

My dad. He's the whole fucking reason Donna and I aren't together. Well, some of it.

I got this phone call. Mom. This is two months after I made parole.

"I tried all day yesterday to reach you," she said. "Your father passed away, Jake." She was trying not to cry way it sounded, without much luck. Every other word was a sniffle.

"I was out," I said. "Looking for a job. When's the funeral?"

I remember looking at my hands to see if they were shaking. They weren't.

When we drove up to the funeral home in South Bend I looked at my watch. One-forty-eight it said in digits. We were supposed to be there at one-thirty.

"Fuck," I said to Donna. In one way I was glad. I didn't want to go to my father's service with a whore. My mother would have picked up on it right away and there would have been something. I just sat in the car in the parking lot, fired up a cigarette. Donna reached over, grabbed my cigarette to light her own.

"How come we're not going in?" she said. "How come you're not a pallbearer?"

"How come you're not Miss Indiana?" I said back. She shut up and moved closer to her own window, blowing smoke out the window.

"Why'm I running this air conditioner when you got the goddamn window open?" I said, when she turned her head.

When the procession started out I turned on my lights and waited for the last car. Then I became the last car. I had no idea which cemetery they were all headed for.

A rent-a-cop came up at the cemetery and asked what I was doing.

"That's my father they're burying over there," I said.

"Oh," he said, like that was fine with him, whatever, and he just stood there awhile by my car door, looking over at the mob of people gathered around the mound of dirt you could see from where we were. Donna still hadn't said anything since the funeral home.

There was a tent set up beside the dirt for those who wanted to get out of the sun. I thought I could see my mother, but we were quite a ways away so, I'm not sure. It looked like her from there, but then I'd never seen her in a black dress or a hat, and she looked different. Maybe it was one of my aunts. From a distance, who knows? The rent-a-cop kept standing there about two feet away, and he just stared at the preacher, even though where we were you couldn't hear anything.

"I didn't know cemeteries had their own police force," I said, trying to keep a conversation from happening. "You lose a lot of bodies?" What was this guy's problem anyway? He muttered something when he saw it wasn't a joke I was making and walked away. I thought he was going to walk over to my father's funeral but halfway there, he made a military turn and went instead toward another funeral that was taking place about two hundred yards away. They were planting them all over the place it looked like.

"Shouldn't you go up or something?" Donna asked.

"Shouldn't you mind your own business?" I shot back. "I might've gone up if we hadn't been so fucking late. If you didn't have to comb your hair forty thousand times we'd been on time." She had nothing to say to that. That was good. I was getting a mood, a real bad one. She wanted to play the dozens I could spot her eleven and still wipe the floor with her ass.

After a while, it was all over. The people started getting back into their cars. It *was* my mother, I saw now. She got in the lead car, the one with the funeral home chauffeur and the little plastic flag, and I think she spotted me. She kind of hesitated, looking our way like she was nearsighted, and then climbed in the back with somebody looked like my Aunt Millie, who was helping her, holding her elbow.

I waited until the last car had left and then I got out and walked toward the big pile of dirt.

There he was in this black coffin. The ropes they'd used to lower him were still there, the ends snaked in esses in the dirt. Yellow shit, looked like clay. I bet the guys dug the graves were glad they had machines to do it now instead of having to use shovels. I stood there for a few minutes looking down at the casket. I just stood there looking and nothing came up in my mind. No thoughts at all, nothing. I looked over at the car and could barely see Donna's head. Looked like she'd laid down in the seat to take a nap, just the top of her head showing where she leaned it against the door.

I just about jumped out of my skin when a voice said, right at my elbow, "Your dad, huh?"

It was that fucking rent-a-cop

"I guess," I said. "My mother got in a limo so it wasn't her. You got a smoke on you?"

He gave me a funny look and then tapped one out of the pack he took from his shirt pocket. He held up his lighter but it kept going out in the breeze. "Here," I said, grabbing it out of his hand. I got it lit after two-three tries, cupping my hand around it.

"How come you didn't go up for the service?" he said. The guy was a nosy cocksucker. I slid my hand in my trouser pocket and felt the knife there. Taking a drag on my cigarette, I looked around. There wasn't anybody around, only the people at the other funeral, and it didn't look like any of them could see us very well. There was a little hill between us and one of those mausoleums in the way, and the few people I could spot weren't looking our way at all.

"You talk too much," I said. I slid the knife out and pushed the button. He saw the knife and his eyes widened.

"Hey, buddy..."

"I got your 'hey buddy' hangin', Ace," I said. "Get the fuck out of my face. Go bother somebody else."

I don't know why I lit the guy up like that. For a minute, I actually thought I was going to zip him. Fucking state trooper wannabe. He walked away very quickly, muttering under his breath when he was far enough away he thought I couldn't hear him.

There wasn't any real reason for even considering shanking this guy or even scaring him like I did but I didn't feel particularly bad about it. Fucking rent-a-cops are zeros anyway. In fact, I felt kind of good about the whole thing. I folded the knife and put it back in my pocket.

I took a deep, last drag on the cigarette and flipped it down on top of the coffin. "There you go, Dad," I said, looking down. "I forgot to bring flowers so I hope this is all right." I spoke aloud, as if he could hear me, and then I started laughing. I couldn't help it.

Well, I said in my head, and then aloud. "Well."

Donna started laying on the horn, a long blast and then another, and then she really laid on it.

"Well, Pappy," I said. "Well, well, well."

Time I got back to the car it was starting to overheat. Steam was curling from the hood. I decided not to check it out there but find a gas station and see what the problem was. I wondered where I was going to spend the night.

SIX

"I was bumrapped, you know."

We were sitting on the balcony of the Seaport Cafe on Bourbon Street in the French Quarter in New Orleans, two hours after we'd driven across the Lake Ponchartrain causeway. Knocking back Pearl beers and shots of Jack, and watching the tourists down below. It was two days before Christmas, four days into our trip South.

Bud was drunk. I'm a sipper, but Bud likes to slam 'em down like it's ten minutes to closing, even if it's high noon.

I'd heard this story a thousand times. Every day in the joint. Every time something would get him down, some hack give him some shit, Bud would trot out his sadsack bumrap tale. Thing was, I knew he was telling the truth.

"I'm fucking this babe," he says and I can finish the story, word for word, I've heard it so much, but I keep quiet and watch the tourists and make like I'm listening. There was a guy in a Santa Claus outfit staggering up the street, a go-cup in his white mitten. It felt about eighty degrees out, so I figured in that outfit it must be near a hundred. Santa must have got into the *good* egg nog, way he was stumbling around.

"I'm fucking this babe, what?—about three-four months, maybe longer. I'm eighteen, she says; that's what she told me a hundred times. I figure she's lying, her boobs were still growing an inch a day, I swear! But I go along with the program. She *acts* eighteen. Hell, in bed, she acts *thirty-eight*. One night, we're done burying the kielbasa for a while, we're up in my crib, and we must've dozed off watching the boob tube. Next thing I know, the door's busting down, and this little bitty guy, couldn't of been nobody else but her old man—same hook nose—comes flying in, bustin' the door down, and starts popping me with this little toy gun. A twenty-two. Fucking shorts. Not even long rifles, pukey-ass shorts. Can you believe that? You believe a guy tries to shoot a guy my size—hell, *any* size—with .22 shorts? Fucker's nuts."

The waiter came by and Bud reached out and grabbed his arm.

"Do it," he said, pointing to our glasses.

The Santa was almost to our block now. I noticed he kept going up to the doors of the strip joints and peeking in. Maybe he was looking for Missus Santa.

"It turns out she's *fourteen*, for crissakes! I knew she wasn't eighteen but I'd've guessed seventeen, maybe the back end of sixteen. But *fourteen?* That freaked me out. Freaked her out, too, way her old man came in like J. Edgar Hoover. Scared her, she started screaming I'd raped her. Came up with this story about how I'd held a knife on her, picked her up at the bus station. She had quite an imagination, I'll give her that. In some ways, I don't blame her. Her father was little, but *scary*, even with that little pissy-ass capgun. She'd already told me some stuff about him, how he useta nail her when she was sleeping, whale the crap out of her, and then make her gobble his knob. I nailed 'im, gave him a shot broke his jaw, but somebody, nosy neighbor prob'ly, had already called the cops."

Bud did his shooter and took a big draw on his beer.

"Yeah, I don't really blame her for what she did. I blame the jury. And the judge. They shoulda seen what was going on, just some little chippy got caught by her daddy and was trying to get out of a mess. She was hard, son," he said, looking at me to see if I was believing him.

I was, and what I was thinking was about all them myths about guys in the joint. Ever time you see a movie about the penitentiary or read a book, there's this thing they got to put in, this bullshit that says everybody doing hard time claims he's innocent. That's pure horseshit. I knew maybe two thousand guys, time I spent in Pendleton and Bud's the *only* one I ever knew said he was innocent. Everybody I ever met in there was *proud* of being an outlaw.

I figured out where that crap come from. Even though nobody claims to be bumrapped—least to other guys inside—you *always* claim you were wrongfully convicted when you talk to straights. I bet Charley Manson does the same thing. You talk to counselors, the parole board, *anybody* but another con, you tell them the system made a big mistake, your case.

So, what happens I figure is the guys that make these movies, they go interview cons for "background," and of course, the guy they talk to says, "Hey, I shouldn't be in here. I'm innocent, man. Was some guy looked like me, my fucking evil twin, maybe." 'Cause the thought is that somebody who has power will believe them and set them free.

Pardons. There's lots of pardons the public don't know about. The governor gives out a couple three-four dozen a year. Big sentences, like the ten and a quarters you get for rape, for residence burglary, they all get cut loose with a pardon from the governor. Six-to-eight, six years, eight months Indiana says you got to serve on a ten and a quarter, and then you're eligible for a pardon. Eighty percent get it first time. You think a guy whose only shot at freedom is a pardon is going to tell somebody, "Yeah, I did it." Yeah, sure. They feed you all this stuff that all they want to see is evidence of remorse, but that's a bunch of bull. Admit you're guilty, you can kiss that pardon good-bye. Long as you get them to thinking there's even a slight doubt of your innocence, you got a shot the governor's gonna sign that paper.

People don't even know this goes on. They think a pardon is only doled out to a couple murderers every hundred years or so. That's the ones make the news. More often as not, there's a big deal in the papers about some guy who's whacked his wife for sharing her love peach but has truly repented for his one slip and wants to rejoin society, as he's a changed man. The newspapers put it out that the governor's really agonizing over it but at the last minute decides he can't, in good conscience, let this poor soul go loose in proper society, as he has to pay the full penalty for the terrible thing he's done. This gets a lot of votes; the straights think, hey, this is one tough hombre we got heading up this state. If they knew he probably just signed a dozen and a half pardon orders to ten-and-a-quarters the day before, they'd shit purple bricks, but that shit never gets in the paper.

There's lots of misconceptions like that. Makes me mad. I give up going to movies about prisons. I haven't seen one yet that come close to the truth.

That's why I believed Bud when he said he was bumrapped. He even said that to all us other cons, which is why I believe him. Even those guys who truly were innocent—and there's some in the joint that are, I know—even those guys would never claim a bumrap to another con. Another con thinks you're not a lifelong hard case he's gonna be all over your ass.

"Yeah, Bud," I said. "I believe you, man."

"Fucking judge," he went on. "Most I shoulda got was statutory rape, give me a one to ten. Asshole judge goes on about how I deflowered this poor little mutt, prob'ly ruined her entire life—shit, she was turning tricks when I met her and rolling half her tricks in a New York second—says the only thing his conscience will let him do is sentence me for first degree, which is the big one."

That's why Bud wasn't on parole. He got one of them pardons after his six-eight the governor gives out like Halloween candy. Cost him five grand, his mom paid and we both know where half of that went, the half the lawyer didn't stick in his own Swiss account. Anybody ever wonders why some sumbitch would spend a million dollars to get elected to a job that pays forty-two G's a year should spend some time in the joint and the math would clear up fast.

Bud was chuckling but it wasn't a laugh of joy. "Little bitch, she's slick. Comes into court wearing this little gingham number with lace on the sleeves and her hair done up in one of them Shirley Temple perms. She had on fucking patent leather shoes. Christ, she looked twelve! I'd been on the jury *I'da* voted to convict. That's what fried my ass."

He went on and on some more but I was shutting him out now. I'd heard the story too many times. Besides, that Santa down below us was fun to watch. He was drunk as a Holstein got in the silage, staggering all over the place, his drink sloshing out of his go-cup, making parts of his suit darker like blood. The sky was the same gray as the sidewalks now and it was cooling off fast. Santa lurched over to a group of tourists, two couples and a little girl belonged to one of them, and reached over and patted one of the women on the ass. I woulda liked to pat her myself. She had on those things used to be called hot pants and she looked hot all right. She let out a little yell we heard clear up where we were, and her husband or boyfriend or whatever clipped Santa, got him right on the button and down he went, his drink spraying every man Jack in the party. There's yelling and screaming and then this cop comes running up. He was in plainclothes like they mostly are in the Quarter, and he puts his foot on

Santa to keep him there and starts talking to the man. Pretty soon—he musta called someone on his beeper—here come two squad cars and they loaded up the whole bunch and took off. Couple of the cops had to whap Santa in the ribs with their sticks first.

"Bet he's out picking sugar cane for the state tomorrow," Bud said, and I grinned.

"Yeah," I said. "Kinda destroys your faith in Santy, doesn't it?"

He looked at me and we both said it at the same time, laughing.

"Not!"

Just then, two lookers walked out from under the balcony we were on, must have been eating inside, and Bud gave out a whistle and they stopped and looked up.

They waited for us to make our way down to the street.

"Those're hookers, you know," I said to Bud. He just grinned.

One of them was a blonde, the kind does it at home in the kitchen sink, the other had a nose that had seen a fist at one time, had the kind of crook you can only get from being broken. Her eyes were striking, though, emerald-green, which really stood out in contrast to her hair, which was so black it had bluish tones to it.

"You're a real flirt, aren't you?" the one with the nose said.

"Fuck a buncha flirting," I said. "Flirting's like driving down cul-de-sacs. You waste a lot of gas and don't never get to where you're goin'. Me, I like to hit the open road and get right to my destination. Run the red lights, all the stop signs if I hafta."

Turned out they were a couple of hookers like I'd thought. And yeah, we got down, had us some fun, copped us each a b.j. in a courtyard off St. Peter's. A couple of times while the ladies were going at it, tourists would pop in, see us and pop right back out. The first time that happened, the girl was with me just turned her head a little to eyeball them and came up for air for just long enough to yell at them, "Fuck off, man. Can't you see I'm working here!"

SEVEN

A couple of days after the Tennessee thing and after our stop in New Orleans there was this little incident in Houma a day before we hit Lake Charles. Houma's this little coonass town that's fulla offshore riggers and such; mean, onery fellas that work the oil rigs out in the Gulf for weeks at a time and then come to town with a pocketful of green and a hard-on that ain't gone anywhere nice in weeks, looking for pussy and fun, fun being the chance to crush somebody's cheekbones into their face with a fist.

We drove into this town at high noon just like Gary Cooper and the OK Corral and spied this bar on the outskirts of town that looked like our kind of place. They had a *wooden* sidewalk. I think they had a wooden sidewalk, but that mighta been another town we stopped in. I guess we stopped in pretty near every place that had a bar. We was pretty drunk that whole time. I said to Bud, let's get us a camera and take a picture a'this!

As I say, it was high noon, *Louisiana* noon, which meant it was brighter outside than a J.C. Penney's White Sale, and we walked in the door and couldn't see a thing for something like two-three minutes; it was that dark. When we could make out objects like tables and a bar and a bartender, we seen that he hadn't had time to do his housekeeping, as there wasn't a *whole* stick of furniture in the place. I mean, tables, chairs, *everything*, was just plain busted up. It looked like a sawmill ten minutes after a wildcat strike.

We go over to the bar and sit down on the only two stools that had a couple-three legs still on 'em, acting like this looked like every bar we've ever been in, and the bartender sauntered over, toothpick sticking out the side of his mouth, and said, in a cocky way, "Y'all ain't Yankees, I hope."

Well, I didn't know it showed, but I went, "Well, pard, I was born in Texas but have lived in Indiana and Chicago and some other places. Does that make me a Yankee? I got to say, though, that I always lived in the south end of town, wherever I was, and that's a fact."

He said, "Me, I don't care what you are, asshole, Chinese for all *I* care, but I got to tell y'all, the riggers're comin back in about an hour."

I looked at Bud and he at me, and I imagine we both had the same question, but before we could articulate it the bar-keep said, "See this mess? The riggers done it. They was in yesterday and they got a little bored smacking each other around so one of 'em bet Whitey he wouldn't coldcock the first person walked in the door, and you know, ol' Whitey, he done it, he's that crazy. Sucker-punched that sumbitch, who was Jeffrey Rousseau—broke his nose—and Jeffrey went out and got his cousins and brothers and in-laws and what-not, which is a considerable bunch a'fellas, and they come in here and done this." He swept his arm to show us, like we hadn't already noticed the A-bomb that had gone off, and this little smile played on his kisser like he was really enjoying himself.

"Those ol' boys went to it and they *broke bones*, Jim. I think they'd like t'fine a couple fellas like y'all here, they come back. In an hour." He looked at his watch and shook his wrist and looked at it again. "Just a friendly warning." He shined us his Kiwanis smile.

I expected Bud to maybe give a snort and order us up a

couple of brewskies, and frankly, I wasn't too hot on that idea, but thank God, he only nodded to the bartender and turned around and headed for the door, me naturally following behind, climbing in the Fairlane and goin' on down the highway, never mind taking a snapshot or two of the wooden sidewalks.

Part-way out of town we seen a liquor store and went in and got us a twelve-pack of Pearl and a bag of ice, and when we got out of town Bud said, pull over on that road over there, which I did, and drove down in the middle of some kind of swamp that looked like the kind Boris Karloff lived in. It was one of them dirt roads didn't look like it got much traffic 'cept on go-to-meetin'-day, run over a snake or an armadillo about ever five yards, and we found a little turn-around place where we could pull off. Bud had stuck his knife in the icebag and rigged up a poor-man's cooler, jamming the beers down in the ice. We kicked the doors open and sat with our backs to each other, legs hanging out onto the ground. Well, Bud stuck his legs out, feet on the ground, but I kept mine up on the floorboard. I could just see some twenty-foot alligator or a mess of water moccasins creeping up under the car and taking a chomp out of my appendage.

"Jake," he said, after we'd chugged down a cold one and had us each a new soldier in hand. "You ever get scared?"

"Well, there's times when I'm more cautious than others, if that's what you mean."

"Fuck it, Jake. I'm askin' you a serious question. You ever been scared of anything?"

Before I could answer, and maybe because he really wanted an answer and knew I wouldn't admit it—having fear, that is—he said, "I been scared most of my life, Jake. You believe that?"

This is a few days after the thing in Tennessee—and after

we'd been in New Orleans—and I thought of that and some other stuff I seen him pull in the joint with some really *bad* dudes.

"Well, Bud, truth is, I was scared pretty much in Pendleton. Not that I was chickenshit," I hastened to add. "You seen me. You know I never backed down to nobody—not even Baby Black Jefferson. Not none of those niggers in J, them weight-lifting sissies, neither."

"Yeah," he said. I couldn't see his face, back to back as we were, but the tone in his voice told me he was somewhere far away in his head.

I started thinking about being scared. Hell yes, I was scared. Every blessed minute of every fucking day. You're not scared in the joint you're dead or terminally stupid.

"What scared you there?" Bud asked, taking a pull on his beer.

I had to think about that.

"Being raped, I guess, was the biggest thing."

"Yeah. There's that. How about somebody going off 'cause their wife just sent them a Dear John and all they wanna do is stick a laundry pin in somebody's eye!"

"Oh, man! I seen that!" I remembered an old con that had happened to. Bud remembered the guy, too, and said so.

"Yeah. Me, too. That old lifer, Mopey Dick we called 'im. Do you know there's blood in an eyeball, not white stuff?"

We both fell silent and sucked our beers.

Then,

"How about not getting your parole, Jake? That's scary, huh?"

"No shit. Or *getting* it and not being able to maintain, on the outside. How about that? I feel that all the time."

"How about syph," he came in with.

"Solitary," I countered.

"That hack, whatshisname? Jacoby? Or Huck? One of the

twins on solitary that like to drop a bench on your nose? Mental defectives!"

"*You're* a mental defective, Bud!"

"Screw you!" He turned around, shook his beer and sprayed it all over my back when I ducked down. We were both laughing but my hands were sweating. We played on. Name The Fear.

"Scared your lady will leave you," started up Bud again.

"Scared she *won't,*" was my offer.

"Scared somebody else will know you're scared."

"Scared you'll find that out about somebody and have to do something about it."

"The train."

Yeah. The train. That was a good one. Every night, this same train would roll by, half a mile away, just on the other side of the wall, and blow his whistle. Fucking whistle used to drive everybody nuts. Guys used to start screaming when that whistle started. First the whistle, then the screams. The screams always used to sound like they came from high up in the cellblock. I don't think I ever heard anybody on the lower levels scream at that train. Cry, though. I heard plenty cry. I heard myself cry. Especially when you heard that whistle and were listening on your earphones to that sad drippy CW shit the prison d.j. liked to play about the same time.

We went through the whole list. It was good, in a way, to know someone else had felt like I had, that I wasn't weird, or weak, or something like that. Bad, too, 'cause it surfaced up a lot of junk I'd forgotten. We just sat there in that swamp and played Name That Fear, and guess what? It felt good. I guess that's 'cause we were out of there.

The fear of going crazy (Bud's).

Fear in the shower (rape—mine); fear in the chow hall (ground glass in the food—a berserk inmate suddenly attacking you—Bud's); fear of betting too much in a cellblock poker game (death for slow-walking on the debt you'll owe—both of us); fear when you shoot up with contraband drugs (who knows what you're really pushing into your arm?—mine); fear on your job (in the barber school, where we were, of who might grab your razor and give you a lower-case smile—mine, again); fear in the recreation yard (rape, maiming—Bud's); fear of the enemy race (blacks for us whites, whites for the blacks—mine); fear of the hacks (some of them were more sadistic than any twenty cons put together—mine); fear in your bunk at night (a black inmate in the cell next to me had acid thrown in his face and screamed all night—mine); fear on visiting day (that no one will show up, or that someone *will* show up—both); fear that the buddy who helps protect you will get paroled (or killed, or horny himself—mine); fear that the hacks will find your shank during a shakedown (loss of parole, loss of your weapon—Bud's). Fear.

A thousand fears, ten thousand fears.

Loneliness. That's just one emotion that's with you always. There are others. Despair.

Jealousy.

Rage.

Other emotions. Lots of other emotions.

Fear of losing yourself, who you are inside.

Fear, man.

I knew now that even as big and bad as Bud was, he had the same fears, maybe even more, since he was a big guy, had a rep, and was therefore subject to being a target more. There's nothing more some guys want than to get them a reputation for taking down someone everyone else knows is bad to the bone. It's kind of like that Indian thing I heard about once, when you kill your enemy you take on his strength.

We drank some more beers and talked about some other

things, mainly about girls; what we'd do to them when we got them, what we'd done other times when we had them, and what they did to us that proved that we was irresistible and incredible lovers. The kind of stuff guys always talk about. I figured out a long time ago that talking about fucking later a lot of times is more fun than the fucking itself was at the time. There have been some incredible fucks I was in the middle of and I remember thinking the whole time she's scratching my back that I can't wait to show somebody what she done. That's weird, but that happens all the time. I'll be laying the wood to some babe and you'd expect I'd be all wrapped up in the here and now, but the truth is what I'm thinking about more than the action is how great it's going to be, telling everybody about it a week from then.

Bud only said one more thing before we killed the twelve-pack and moved on. He said, "Sometimes I get so scared, I get the bravest I ever been. That's what it was like back there in Tennessee. When I seen that guy's eyes, I knew if I couldn't Jeff Chandler his ass I was dead."

Don't that beat all! He sure had me fooled is all I could think, only I didn't say that to him. What I said to him was, "Yeah, right." Then he laughed and I laughed, too, but something happened because of what he said. I got a little scareder inside...and I got a little gutsier at the same time. I can't tell you how that works but it felt just like that.

Something else Bud said made sense to me. That part about being so scared you get brave. I did that so much in the joint that right before I made parole I was brave all the time. Guts out the whazoo. I wasn't scared of nothing. It only lasted a little while, until I walked out the front gate, parole papers in my hand. As soon as free air hit my lungs, the greatest feeling of fear I had ever known washed over me. But for the month or so before I hit the bricks I was the cockiest mother in the joint.

The minute I took my first free breath when I walked out the front door something else hit me. Lots of older cons were all the time saying they'd rather do straight time than be on the street on parole, and I thought: That's just jail talk, bullshit. How can anybody in their right mind think it's better to do ten years inside than five in and five out on parole? Shit, you're on parole, sure, and things aren't the same when you're on parole as when you're a regular citizen, but cut me a break—you'd rather do the five inside so when they cut you loose you're totally free? I used to ask those guys that and they said, we know, we know, it sounds nuts but that's the way we feel. When I walk out I want to be completely free, they'd say. Nobody fucking with my shit is freedom, they'd say, and I'd think, you're wacko, friend.

But they weren't. I saw that the second my foot hit the pavement and they closed the door behind me. All of a sudden I knew I was going to have this asshole watching every move I made. Every time I took a shit I was going to have to fill out a report, fuck; call and get permission before I even sat on the crapper. At least in the joint you do what you want mostly. Hacks leave you alone you do your time in a righteous way.

I still didn't agree all the way but I could see their point. Parole to some guys is worse than time in solitary. There's always that little parole officer genie shithead sitting on your shoulder the whole time.

I thought about all that shit on the bus ride home, first time I got cut loose on parole, but in the end I just said fuck it, no matter what you do, no matter what your situation, you end up doing time. The freest cocksucker in the world has probably got a wife got his nuts in a wringer, afraid to look at her cross-eyed and lose his pussy, or else got him a boss who's got him kissing his big fat ass so he keeps his lousy job. Everybody's got a parole officer of some kind, I guess.

Best thing is to get on a desert island someplace, jack off and eat oysters all day long, fuck everybody in the universe. Then you be free, man. You're in control.

EIGHT

Out of the blue Bud said, "I wonder what Kimmie's doin right now?"

Fuck. Like I needed that. Immediately, a picture of Donna popped up and I had half a mind to turn the car around and head north. In a few minutes the feeling passed. At least it died down to a manageable ache.

This fucking swamp went on forever! The locals must use another highway, 'cause I bet there hadn't been a car by on the other side in more than ten minutes. I kept thinking, we have us a flat and they'll have to cut some gator open to find enough to bury by the time help arrives. Just before we got to the highway, Bud said, pull off up there, I got to take a piss.

Soon's he hit the bushes he started yelling.

I jumped out of the car quick, opened the trunk and took out the Mossberg. Gator's got him is what I thought. Maybe a snake.

It wasn't neither. When I reached him, he was just standing there, holding his pizzler, a look on his face like somebody'd just told him his best dog got run over.

"Jake," he said and there was some serious stress in his voice. "Jake, I…" He looked up at me and I could see the pain pinching his mug. "I got me a dose. It's a bad one, Jake. Worst I ever had, bro. Oh me, oh my, it *hurts*."

It looked like he'd been peeing on a log mighta been an alligator.

"Teach you to always grab the best-lookin' one," I said. "That cross-eyed gal I had was sorta ugly but least I don't sound like James Brown crankin' out a hit when I make water. Bud, I think you might wake up that log you're peein' on. I believe I seen some eyes on it."

I didn't laugh but I couldn't keep from grinning when he jumped back.

"First town we hit we'll get you a doctor, partner."

"You think this is funny, Jake?" I guess he seen me smile. Try as I did, I just couldn't wipe that sucker off my face. "You might have a case yourself, you know."

I hadn't thought about that. Shit.

The speed limit was sixty-five but I kept it pegged at just under eighty.

"Lake Charles" said the sign, and we found a doctor on Calcasieu Boulevard. He give Bud the biggest shot I ever saw and drew blood from both of us. "Don't drink any beer," he said. We had to go back that afternoon when the blood tests came back. "I don't need bloodwork on you but I'll take one anyway," he said to Bud. "My dog could diagnose you. See how he went to the other side of the room when you came in?" There was one'a them little Pomeranians in the doctor's chair when we walked into his office and sure enough, when Bud stepped over to pet him he ran into the corner and stood there shaking all over like someone had just stepped on and crushed his paw. "Are you allergic to penicillin?" the doc said, grinning.

We drove around looking for a place to kill some time until we could see if I was infected, too. About four blocks from the doctor's office there was the biggest black cow we ever saw, about fifteen feet tall. *Black Angus,* said the sign on the building. *Cold Beer,* it said, under. We got us a place at the bar, which wasn't hard as we were the only customers.

Half-hour later I went to take a dump. Just as I was

getting comfortable I heard Bud come in. I knew it was him by his moans.

"Told you not to drink that beer," I called out. "Doctor told you, too."

"Fuck you," he said. "I'm gonna go in a bar and not have a beer? Just shut up, Jake. I got problems enough without you up my ass. I think you got a worse disease than I do, buddy. Something crawled up inside you and died. Think that doctor has a shot for what you got?"

I swear I heard him bending the plumbing, only it was hard to tell over his groans.

Then I heard another voice, not Jake's.

"I want to thank y'all for making this easy." What the fuck? I thought, but before I could say anything, the door to the stall burst open and there stood a little guy couldn't have been much over five-foot-tall, bald-headed, looked like an accountant, stood there grinning at me. He was a little guy but the gun he was holding was good-sized. Looked like every inch of a .357.

"My friend, I want you to ease off that stool and lay down on the floor on your stomach." He waved the gun over where I knew Bud was standing. "You, too, big guy. Lay down on the floor by your partner."

This was humiliating. My butt was sticking up in the air and I could feel shit oozing out where I'd broken off my crap. My nose was picking up the smell of piss on the floor. I lay beside Bud, who was already down when I crawled out of the stall like a crab.

"You don't smell so pretty good," the bandit said. He walked over and took out my wallet and then Bud's. "I'm a nice guy," he said, opening the door. "I just want your money. I'm gonna leave you your wallets." He tossed them on the floor beside us after he lifted out the bills. "Come out before I git gone y'all'l be making a big mistake. Adios, amigos." The door wheezed shut and we heard the click of his heels outside on the linoleum.

"Come *on*," Bud said, standing up and zipping his fly. "He's gonna get away."

There was no way I was pulling up my shorts over a shitty ass. "Hold your horses. I'm wiping before I leave. Sucker's gone anyway," I said. "Don't wait for me," I said. "Go on out, see if he means what he says. Fucker's long-gone, Bud."

He was. We ran through the bar to the front and out to the car, looking down the street both ways. I flipped the keys to Bud and he unlocked the trunk and fetched out his pistol.

"Put that in your pocket," I said, looking around to see if anyone had noticed the man waving a pistol. Luckily, we were alone. "You crazy?"

He stuck it in his belt and pulled his shirt out of his pants to cover it.

"Let's check the rest of the parking lot," he said. You could see all of it from where we stood but we looked anyway, peeking under cars.

Back inside we inventoried the damage. There was the change on the bar from the round Bud had bought. Sixteen bucks and a couple of quarters. I had a twenty in my sock, Bud nada, zip, zero.

"Thirty-six stinkin dollars," Bud said. "This just ain't right."

The bartender was standing there looking at us. It occurred to me he didn't have the foggiest what had just happened in his bar.

"Let's call the cops," Bud said.

"We can't," I said, the voice of reason.

"What? Why the fuck not?"

"Think about it, Bud. I broke parole. You think that's a wise move, calling the cops? Cops like to check up on people, even victims. They got these computers they love to use."

"Well, *fuck*. You mean I got to lose my money just because you did a stupid thing like break parole? You think that's fair?"

He was just mad. I gave him a couple of minutes to think about it and calm down. He knew what being partners meant when it come down to it. He drank down the rest of his beer and mugged at the wall for a couple of minutes and then he said, "You're right. We can't call the cops. Wouldn't do much good anyway. Guy's long gone by now. He's a pro."

The bartender came up.

"Got a problem?"

"Yeah," said Bud.

"No," I said. "Everything's fine and dandy. 'Cept I need a job. Need another bartender?" One thing you learn when you outlaw for a living, you get a loss you cut it loose and go on. Nothing's gained by crying about what might have been. Time for that shit when you're old and sitting in a rocking chair and don't have nothing else much to do 'cept think about couldabeens.

Bartenders they was flush with, the guy said, "But you might could get on as a swamper. Guy we had quit just last night. Boss's running an ad today. He's in the back. Hang on, I'll ask him."

Turns out I was in the right place at the right time. The boss, Mr. Fryin Pan-ee, sounded like, one of those French names, hooked me up with an apron on the spot and a locker in the kitchen, gave me the lowdown on the job, which didn't take five minutes. Roll over the tables, clean 'em off when the parties leave, take out the garbage for the cooks, help out on the service bar when things got busy, any kind of shit work cook needs done, or the waitresses. Everybody's your boss. The Black Angus was a steak and dance place, got busy at night when the families cleared out, he said, the bartender nodding. Every time Mr. Fryin Pan-ee said something, the bartender, name of Joe, nodded his head up and down like the bossman was Elvis and he was one of the roadies.

"This is the hot spot in town," the boss said. "We got us a killer band here, plays a lot of Seegar stuff. You get minimum wage and the waitresses give you part of their tips. I catch you stealin' I cut your nuts out. Don't be fucking with the waitresses and definitely don't be fucking with the customers. I catch you fucking with the customers, I cut your nuts out."

There was some other general rules and regulations, same as you get anywhere, and the penalty for each transgression seemed to be, "Do that and I cut your nuts out."

I looked at Bud and he at me, and I know we was both thinking the same thing—this guy's got a thing for jean beans.

Going out the door—I had two hours before I had to report back for the night shift—Bud said, "You think he's queer? He sure talks a lot about dicks and stuff."

"Nuts, Bud. He didn't say nothing about dicks. Just nuts."

Bud grinned. "Oh, he's a bisexual."

Going back to the doctor to see if I had the clap was out of the question now. He'd expect to be paid and I didn't want to chance what he'd do if we didn't take care of the bill, being strangers and all. And Yankees.

First night we slept in the car out along the Dismal Swamp. We were both broke-dick dogs. Me from working my ass off, cleaning greasy plates and generally running around like I was in training for the Kitchen Olympics and Bud from the tenseness of his condition.

His condition put work on the backburner far as Bud was concerned. He looked, sorta, but couldn't find anything. Almost got a job in a warehouse but the straw boss smelled booze on him and that was that. To be fair, he didn't feel much like working. It was about all he could do, anticipating the next time he had to take Willie out. That kept his mind off employment, minor things like that. I told him, quit drinking beer like the doc said, you don't have to go as often. It was all right, though. I was making enough for us both to get by.

The first day I sold my Mossberg and rifle to the night manager, Mexican guy named Jose, at the Angus and got us enough to get a cheap motel. Jose musta took a shine to me 'cause he took me aside and told me he'd pay me cash every night first week, so's we could get set up. It was tight, but it worked out and we began to settle in. I was going to go for a barber's job as soon as we could get Louisiana licenses, only I had forgot about the parole violation thing and happily remembered it before I did something stupid, like apply for a license, have my ass show up on the Crime Computer Network, whatever they called it.

One thing I did, soon as I knew we had a place to stay and a few bucks. I went down and bought a postcard at a drugstore. It was a picture of Lake Charles—there was a lake in the middle of town that had the same name as the town—it was a picture off this bridge going over it and water-skiers and folks doing family shit like that down below—and I sent it off to Donna.

I wrote on the back: "Dear Donna, How are you? I am fine, down here in the Deep South. I have got a position at a fine restaurant and night club. They made me an assistant manager right off. You'd be proud of me. I miss you. I tried to kill myself. Ha. Ha. I have been thinking about you and still love you, Donna. I hope we can still have a future." I signed it, "Best Wishes and All My Love, Jake."

I thought a minute, sucking on the ballpoint top, then added:

"P.S. You shouldn't of done that to the baby."

NINE

Dumb, dumb, dumb!

First rule of scoring with the ladies: Don't make the first move.

Second rule: If you break the first rule, forget the lady and go on to someone new. She's got you by the short hairs and you're in for a long, rough ride of heartache and misery.

I didn't care. Try as I could, I just couldn't shake Donna, get her out of my mind. I had to face it, she owned me, my mind anyway, and whatever else you got will follow what goes on upstairs. Time after time, I thought on it and kept coming up with the same thought. I'd rather be miserable with or without her than be happy with someone else. Dumb? Sure. But your dick ain't got an I.Q. and neither does your heart. Maybe they're one and the same, sometimes I guess they are, and sometimes they aren't. I mean, I think that thing everybody calls love is maybe just more than sex, although sometimes that's all it is but there were times, like with Donna, I could just lay there looking in her brown eyes and not even be thinking about sex with her, just wanting to smell her breath. She has this little chip on one of her front teeth that drives me crazy. I'd lay on the floor staring at her, both of us stretched out and just mug for hours into those eyes, the whole time aching for a peek at that tooth. I knew all I had to do was crack a joke and she'd smile and I'd see it, but I'd play it out forever, holding back the jokes, whatever, until I couldn't stand it any longer, and then, man! I couldn't hold back any longer, would say something funny and she'd grin, and there was that tooth with that tiny little chip in the corner. In some ways, that kind of stuff was ten times better'n sex. Man! Sometimes I don't even understand my own screwy self.

"Who you sending that to?" Bud said, when I got back in the car. "That broad's got you all fucked up?"

"Sometimes you got a big nose," I said.

"Good thing I ain't got big tits," he came back with. "You'd be mailing me love notes all'a time, then."

I got home the next morning there was a dog in my bed. A fucking German shepherd, big as a sofa.

"Get the fuck out of there!" I yelled at him and grabbed the skin on his neck and pulled him off. He didn't want to come but I got him down.

"Where the hell did this dog come from?" I screamed at Bud, laying on the other bed. He was smoking a doobie. I didn't ask him where he got it or where he got the money for it. Should have figured he was holding out on me but for some reason it didn't piss me off. That dog did, though. I hate friggin' dogs. Ever since that time at the Out of Towner Motel in South Bend when the cop sicced his mutt on me after I was cuffed. Fucking dog bit my back through a jacket, a wool shirt, a T-shirt and I lay on my stomach for two days in the cell before they sent me over to the hospital for stitches.

"I don't know," Bud said, staring at the TV where an old Lucy show was going on, Lucy and Ethel on some kind of production line, dressed up in white chef's hats and aprons, and the cupcakes or whatever they were supposed to be icing, going haywire, falling off the line all over the place. "He was outside the door and seemed hungry, so I let him in. He likes beer."

Plus, he's got the radio on. Some Top Forty bullshit. I hate Top Forty. I'd rather listen to country, hillbilly shit than Top Forty. Talk radio. I'd rather listen to talk radio. I turned it off and Bud didn't even seem to notice.

The goddam dog was stoned, I could see that in a second, and kept wanting to sniff my crotch. I hate that, stupid dogs.

"His name's Spot."

I looked at the dog and gave him the knee, as he was trying for my balls again. I didn't see any spots on him. He was mostly dark brown with a gray ring around his neck, and he had one blue eye and one brown one. Fucked-up looking dog if you ask me. Now he was trying to lick my face. Disgusting things, dogs. First they lick your balls and then they try to lick your face. Makes you really want to hang with a dog, you know?

"Hey, don't hurt him," Bud said, when I kicked Spot in the slats. The dog didn't even whimper even though I cracked him pretty good. Must have been used to being kicked. Bud whistled, or tried to; it was a pretty sick whistle, and the dog went over to him. He scratched his ears and talked baby talk to him. It's disgusting, the way some people are with dogs. This dog smelled, too. He was making my stomach roll.

"Dogs are better'n broads, Jake, you know that? You gotta talk to broads after you fuck them, entertain 'em. You talk to dogs, they don't talk back, give you any shit, they listen to you like you're God. Hey, wouldn't it be great, find a babe like that!"

I thought about saying, Yeah, well you got a dog already, name of Kimmie, but I didn't. Say that, that is. It was true though. Bud's girlfriend kind of looked like this dog. I wondered if he scratched Kimmie's ears, talked baby talk to her. Maybe I'd ask him sometime. Sometime when I wanted a black eye.

"I hate dogs," I said, and went into the bathroom to get a

beer. We still hadn't got a cooler, although we'd talked about it. Just kept the beer in the sink, got ice for it every once in a while from the motel ice machine down the hall. I saw there was something blue on the ice and then figured out Bud must have brushed his teeth. I rinsed the can of beer a long time before I popped the top.

"I had a dog just like this once," Bud was saying, still slobbering over the mutt, kissing him back on the muzzle. Yech!

"Belonged to Marty Simmons." he said. "You know Marty? He was the inmate librarian at Pendleton when we was there. We got cut loose the same time but Marty didn't even last a day on the streets."

He was wrestling with the dog now, which I didn't appreciate much. It made him smell even worse. The dog, not Bud. Well, Bud, too. Bud went on about Marty Simmons.

"We get off the bus in Fort Wayne and Marty's not there five minutes he swipes a newspaper from the stand. Course, with his luck the lady behind the counter spies him and calls the cops, and there musta been a coffee shop just around the corner 'cause they were there in twenty seconds flat. I offer to pay for the paper but they must have had a hard on 'cause they say fuck no, we're taking him in. Get us another ex-con off the streets, says the other one, his partner. 'Bud,' Marty says to me, they're leading him away in cuffs. 'Go by my old lady's house and get my dog. She says I don't show up and get him she's taking him to the pound.' Well, I did what he said, went by his old lady's house—it was only three blocks away like he said—and sure enough she had this German shepherd she was taking care of till Marty got out. He was right, too—she said he didn't come by that very day she was shipping him off to the pound. I got the dog and took him home. Great pet. Had that dog for almost six months before he got hit by a bus."

"So how come Simmons didn't get him when he got out?" I couldn't believe stealing a newspaper would keep Marty behind bars for long.

"Oh, he got whacked. In the jail. They were just about ready to cut him loose—they just wanted to fuck with him a little on account of him being an ex-con. When I went down there to see if he was getting cut loose, the cop who'd busted him, the little one, was there. He was laughing. Said Simmons was dead, wouldn't be snatching any more newspapers. Seems he got iced by a big fag-junky who got offended when Marty didn't want to get romantic. Cut his throat with a double-edge razor blade match-welded onto a toothbrush."

We'd both seen that little trick plenty of times.

"You know how it is in city lockup, Jake. Jail's fucking worse than the joint, kind of trash you get in there."

He was right on with that statement. The problem with jails, city, county, it don't matter, is that lots of the guys you run into have just been thrown in there and are still drunk or high or whatever. In the joint, most of the guys have settled down, got the chemicals out of their system. Plus, there's ways to avoid trouble, better than there is in most lockups where everybody's put together in one big bullpen.

"So anyway, I end up keeping Marty's dog. His name was Spot, too. I seen this dog and it was like deja vu. Maybe it's the original Spot, looks a lot like him. You think dogs get reincarnated like Hindus do?"

I didn't know and I didn't care. I couldn't say much, though. The room was half Bud's.

"Just keep him the fuck away from me," I warned. "And give him a bath. He stinks."

There was something on Bud's mind he wanted to talk about, it seems. He was getting antsy. Unable to find work, unable to work, even if he did find something, he laid around the motel room all day. He couldn't even drink beer with the dose he was getting over. Only he did. The doc had said the symptoms might last a couple or three days. He drank anyway, or tried to. Swig down two-three swallows and then he'd be in the john, sweat popping out on his forehead when he tried to squeeze a few drops out. I was getting tired of his bitching and moaning all the time. Now, if it wasn't Bud whining, it was the dog. Picture all this in a room not much bigger than my cell back in the joint. I guess I was getting testy.

"You an alcoholic, Bud? Just lay off that stuff another day or two and you'll be fine. Wise up. Listen to what the doc told you. Take your dog out for a run, make you feel better. A good long run, maybe for about a week. See if you can lose him maybe.

"Fucking dogs, anyway. My first bust a dog fucked me up. We'd just hit a bar—I think it was the fifth or sixth place that night, and we've got TV's, cases of whiskey, rolls of quarters, all kinds of shit in the car. That was a great car, too." I stopped my story for a minute, thinking about that car. It was a sixty-two T-bird, burgundy, with a white leather interior. Class machine.

"It's about four in the morning and we decide to call it quits. I'm taking Rat and DuWayne home and I was stopped at a red light at the corner of Ironwood and Lincoln Way, going south.

"This car comes around the corner behind us, back where Martin's Supermarket is. and the light is flashing. It could have just been a taillight out or something like that, but with all the stuff in the car I didn't feel like taking a chance. Besides, this was when the South Bend Police Department had all the Larks. Remember that?"

Somebody sapped the South Bend P.D. into buying these Studebaker Larks for patrol cars. Anybody remembers the

Lark remembers they were total dogs on wheels. Six-bangers that could get up to fifty with a good tailwind maybe so long's they had twenty minutes to unwind. Outlaws all over town, professionals *and* amateurs, had a field day with those pooches. Kids would squeal their tires in front of one of them and pull away in second gear. The cops hated them. Couldn't catch a bicycle with more than two speeds. The chief of police that okayed buying them got laughed out of office next election and they just scrapped the whole entire fleet, bought Fords with Police Interceptors under the hood. It was nice while it lasted, though. Sweet.

"I took off from this turkey and hit the railroad track across the street—you know where it goes almost straight up?—and went airborne on the other side. I got a look at the speedometer just before we hit the top of that hill and it was already pegged over a hundred.

"We come down and all you seen was sparks, but I kept my foot on the gas and we're going down the street at one-twenty, although it coulda been faster—that's just what it said on the speedometer.

"Ironwood narrows down there because of the residential neighborhood, stop signs every single block but I run them all.

"That's when DuWayne—he's in the back seat—starts screaming, 'Let me out! Let me out!' I look back and he's got tears running down his cheeks and I said, 'Hey, DuWayne, there's the door. You want out, go ahead.'

"I tell Rat and him to get down on the floor and DuWayne hits it so fast I thought he went out the door after all, but he only fell to the floor crying and sobbing like he probably did when he was two and somebody stole his lollipop. I think he peed his pants, too. There was something in the air wasn't burning rubber.

"All this time we're smoking down Ironwood. I got the

peg buried and the cop is so far behind us I can't even hardly see his lights anymore. Just then I see red lights up ahead of us, reflected in the sky.

"'They called ahead,' Rat says, like I can't see the same thing he does. 'This is close to my house,' he says. 'Turn there! I'll get us out of here.' Only it's not the right street—it's a dead end, which we find out at the end of a very long block, and now we can see the flashes of the cops' lights, and they're close.

"We got to hit it on foot," I said. "Grab what you can." We all hit the silk. I grabbed a money bag had rolls of quarters and took off across a lawn. I could see a woods behind it. Where Rat and DuWayne went I didn't have a clue. Time like that it's every man for himself.

"Way it turned out, I get behind this house and into this woods and through it and I'm in this big-ass field with another woods in front of me, and that's what I'm heading for, and I hear this heavy breathing and footsteps behind me, and it's Rat.

'Where's DuWayne?' I ask, and Rat doesn't know, he just took off after me and has just now caught me. His house where he lived with his mother is about three miles straight ahead in the direction we'd been running. We decided to head for there. DuWayne and I were staying at the Out of Towner Motel just a couple of blocks away.

"We kind of ran, then walked, then ran some more and along the way we came up with a plan. We'd get our butts to Rat's house, get out of our clothes, which were soaked, and pick up his car—this was winter and there was about a foot of snow on the ground—then head over to the Out of Towner, see if DuWayne had made it there and then we figured we'd head to New York. We figured there was so many criminals in New York they wouldn't even bother looking for three small-time burglars from Indiana.

"We got to Rat's house okay, and his mom never even woke up. She's a stone alkie so I guess she was in her usual coma. We got our wet clothes off and grabbed some of Rat's and put them on and went out and climbed in his car.

"Drive by the motel first," I told Rat. I didn't think there was any way the cops would know where we were staying, but there was no sense in taking chances. We pulled into the all-night gas station next to it and filled up, and then just pulled across the drive into the motel's parking lot.

"There was a guy downstairs at the desk, looked like he'd fallen asleep reading a magazine. He woke up for a second when we came in and then just nodded and started pretending to read his magazine again, like he hadn't been asleep on duty.

"We walked upstairs to where our room was and I dug in my pocket looking for my key. Rat kind of pushed on the door and it opened a little bit. I looked at him and pushed the door wider. I couldn't see a thing, as it was dark inside. DuWayne? I said, taking a step inside. See, I was thinking somehow DuWayne had beat us back and was sitting inside, probably shaking in his boots and wondering what in the hell he was going to do next.

"Then, BOOM! All hell bust loose. There were guys all over Rat and me, like stink on shit, and I was down on the floor on my knees when somebody smacked me in the back of the head and then somebody else was kicking me, and there was this fucking German shepherd chawing at my arm. It was the cops, only it took a couple of seconds before I realized what had happened. I found out later that stupid-ass DuWayne had never even tried to make a run for it. Just sat in the car and waited for the cops. They found the motel key in his pocket and had it all staked out long before we even got there. At least that's what he said, later. I kinda think he just rolled over on us.

"Well—now this is the part I'm getting to, about why I don't like dogs, Bud—they get us cuffed up after they smacked us around a little—you ever been busted when they didn't hit you? I never have. They always have to whale on you. Makes 'em feel tough, I guess, to beat up on somebody's got handcuffs on. Major macho cop shit.

"They've got me cuffed behind my back and on my knees and bent over this couch is out in the hallway. And the German shepherd is biting my back. I've got a jacket on, a sweater, a flannel shirt and an undershirt, and this fucking dog goes through that like it's the wrapper on a Hershey bar. I'm getting nailed by this dog—fuck, I can *feel* the blood running down my sides—and these asshole cops are laughing. Finally, when they get enough jollies watching me get eaten alive by this mutt, they jerk me up and start downstairs.

"They're taking us downstairs to the squad car, and I've got my hands cuffed behind me, and this dog is trying to eat my cojones. The cop that's dragging me is laughing and lets me in on the fact that these dogs are trained to go for the nuts or the throat. I'm walking like I'm spastic, trying to keep Rover from munching on the crown jewels, and they think it's a riot.

"Finally we get to the car and they put the dog in the back seat with me. Two of the cops climb in the front; all the time this dog's growling and taking nips out of my leg. 'This is Joe,' the one cop says, meaning the dog—he's talking to me—'and he just graduated from obedience school. At the bottom of his class. He's hard to control, that dog is.' They both hoot it up at that.

"Anyway, I'm in the St. Joe County Lockup and I got to lay on my stomach for two days before they send me to the hospital to get stitches. My back's infected and this doctor doesn't believe in wasting Novocain on degenerates like me when he's sewing them up, so what I'm telling you, Bud, is—I-HATE-FUCKING-DOGS—especially German-fucking-shepherd dogs, which is what that one over there is, and this one looks exactly like that dog Joe that did this to me."

I showed him my back, the scars, but he didn't seem very sympathetic. He did try and keep Spot away from me the rest of the night. I don't think it was my welfare he was concerned with though. I think Bud was more worried about his mongrel mutt and what I might do to him.

"I been thinking," he said the next night, finally bringing up what was bothering him. I kind of had an idea what was coming, things he'd been saying. "This sucks, this place."

"It'll get better," I said. We were laying back on the beds watching the tube, sucking on beers. The mutt was behaving for once, laying down on the floor beside Bud's bed. A great movie, "The Hustler," one of my all-time favorites, was on. Paul Newman was doing some shots I wanted to try myself. Both on the table and back at his apartment with the broad he was shacked up with. Little crippled broad when she was walking around, an Olympic athlete when she laid down. "We get ahead some, things'll look rosy again. Hang in there, pard."

"No," he said, swinging his legs around and standing up. "No, it won't. I can't stand this place, Jake. Everybody talks like a hillbilly, can't understand them."

"They *are* hillbillies," I said, snorting. "*I* think they sound kinda cute. You're just pissed 'cause you can't nail one, bein's you got a tragic disease." I wasn't doing too hot in the romance department, either. Seems none of the gals I met at work wanted much to do with a swamper. Mostly, they treated me like I was retarded or something.

"I'm going back, Jake. I'm gonna go call Kimmie, see if she'll let me move back in."

There was no talking him out of it. His mind was made up. I seen, after arguing for just a little bit, trying to talk him out of it, that this was something he'd been thinking on for a while. I gave up, said fuck it.

"Hey, you gotta go, you gotta go."

One thing you learn quick in the hustle game is not to get attached to anyone. We all move around, scuffle here and there. There's no marriages nor partnerships made in heaven the way we live. Bud was a good pard and we'd hook up again someday, I figured. That was another thing. Partners come and they go, and when you meet up again, it's like you just seen them the day before—even if it's been maybe ten years since you've run into 'em. That's the nice thing about being in our corner of society—your friends are friends for life, whether you see them every day or not. Same way with your enemies. Guys are all the time grudge-fucking somebody.

All I could do was wish Bud luck, which I did.

Once he made up his mind, it didn't take long to put his plan into motion. All he had to do was throw his stuff in his suitcase and I was driving him down to the Greyhound station, next morning. Guys like us didn't stand on ceremony and sit around and suck our thumbs. We decided something, we did it. Just like that.

"Kimmie gave me a ration," he said when he came back from calling her, "but she come around. I told her how much I missed her sweet lovin' and she like to make me come over the phone. You get back to the Fort, give me a call. I'll be at the old popstand."

I give him twenty bucks and he bought a bottle of Jim Beam, a fifth, and a oyster po-boy at the shop across from the station, and he was set in style for his ride back to Indiana.

"What you gonna do about your dog?" I wanted to know. We'd left him back at the motel with a water dish full of beer.

"Shit. I don't know. I forgot about him. Tell you what, you take care of him. Just for a day or so. I get back to Fort Wayne I'll send some money, you put him on a plane or something. Just be a few days."

Sure, you bet, I thought, but didn't say anything, just nodded. He couldn't hold me to any promise I hadn't actually made.

"I'll think about you when the snow's ten feet deep up there," I said, and we shook hands, and he swung up the steps, and that's the last I seen him; they had those smoked windows on the bus where you can't make any of the passengers out.

I felt kind of sad but that's the way it goes. You don't stand in anybody's way any more than you'd want them to stop you from what you wanted to do. That's what makes a pard better than a wife, any day.

Soon as I got back to the motel room, I collared the dog and drug him out to the car. The best place I found was that swamp we slept by the first night in town.

"Go on," I said, giving him a little kick. The mutt trotted forward a few feet and sat down on his haunches and looked at me. "Bye-bye, Spot," I yelled out the window. "Go find yourself a big alligator to play with."

That night I got lucky, got a girl, one of the waitresses, to come back to the motel with me, and then I felt better about things.

This girl, her name was Nancy, but everybody just called her Sugar, was one sweet cookie in bed and we had us a good time and all...but I couldn't help thinking about Donna the whole time. It musta been because Bud had left for Indiana made me think about the folks back there, her especially.

Sugar left, said she had to get back before her husband came rolling in from his nightly drunk and as soon as she left, I picked up my notebook and a pen and began writing.

"Dear Donna," I began and damned if I wasn't stuck for something to say.

Finally I put down, "I have tried to get you out of my mind but that is the IMPOSSIBLE DREAM. How about you? Do you think of YOURS TRULY ever?" Once I got going the writing came easy. I ended up with about six pages of mostly mush, which is a lot for me. I tried not to talk about her stabbing Patsy and all that stuff, just tell her how I felt about her. After I sealed it shut, I put the stamp on upside down, wondering if she'd catch that.

About the only stupid thing I didn't do was put S.W.A.K. on the dumb envelop.

Then I ran down to the mailbox on the corner and mailed it before I came to my senses.

I guess I got it bad.

Then, to make it worse, I hear something at the front door, sounds like scratching. Four a.m. in the morning it was. It was that cocksucking dog, Spot. A regular Lassie-come-home. I went back in and tried to ignore him but he kept on scratching and then whining and then just regular barking. I let him back in, gave him some beer and some of the fries from MacDonald's me and Sugar hadn't eaten, and he scarfed it down and jumped up on Bud's bed.

"Tomorrow," I said. Like I was talking to a regular person. "Tomorrow we're gonna take a long ride. A real long ride."

God! That dog sure smelled! Like somebody's old socks, only worse.

TEN

I got rid of Spot the next night.

How? Simple. I pulled a burglary, took him with me. Left him there.

I was tired of being broke.

It was just some gin joint I'd seen, the other side of town. Piece of cake getting in. Taped this little window on the back door, smashed it with a brick, reached in and unlocked the door. Found the money in about twenty seconds in the dirty towel hamper. I took the money, exactly two hundred bucks, must of been the change money for the next day. Bartenders all over the country hide their money in the same places. If it ain't in the dirty laundry, look in the trash can. There was a case of Jack Daniels in the back room I grabbed and toted out to the car. Spot was in the back seat, whimpering like he thought I'd left him for good again. He came right with me, didn't even have to whistle or anything. Followed me right back into the bar and once we were inside, I took a dirty bar rag, waved it under his nose and then threw it across the room. "Fetch, numb-nuts," I said and he went after it. I was still laughing ten minutes later when I unlocked my motel room and went in.

I kept laughing at the thought that he was an accessory and the way cops were they might even send him to trial. I started imagining some wacky scenes.

Spot would stand trial and then they'd send him to some

boot camp joint out in the parish where they had Vietnamese prisoners. There was Vietnamese all over Lake Charles. There was a guy taught out at the college, McNeese State, wrote some book about them, won that big writing award, the Pulitzer Prize. He come in the Angus and one of the waitresses pointed him out, told me all about him. Bud's dog, though, I pictured in my mind, some gook, working in the kitchen, would see this mutt and his eyes would glaze all over and before you knew it, Spot would be in the sweet 'n sour pork.

Couldn't happen to a more deserving mutt, I thought, snickering aloud to myself in the motel room.

The next day I phoned Bud at Kimmie's. He was there, answered the phone himself.

"Hey," he said, first thing. "I ran into your parole officer. There's a guy would like to have your address."

He hadn't told him anything, of course.

We talked about nothing for a while and he brought up my parole officer again. Delbert Brooks. He was an okay guy for a P.O., got on your case a lot less than most of the others. There was one, James Finn, who liked to brace his parolees each time they came in, shake them down. Fucking queer, we all decided, just liked to cop a feel off his guys. I was glad I had Brooks and not Finn. I don't know what I'd do if I had Finn and he shook me down, felt my ass like I've seen him doing. Bust him, probably, smack him. Maybe not. It wouldn't be worth it, have him violate you, send you back. Wait for him in some alley would be better. Stick him when he wasn't looking.

"Brooks says I see you, let you know if you were to come back in the next week or so he wouldn't violate you."

I'd have to go to a halfway house, Bud said, but Brooks wouldn't send me back to Pendleton.

"You believe him?" I asked.

"Yeah. I do, Jake. Brooks is all right. Straight-up guy."

Bud was right. I'd never heard anything but that Brooks was all right. If he said he wouldn't violate me, he wouldn't violate me. But did I want to go back to Indiana? Part of me wanted to because of Donna, and part of me didn't want to. Because of Donna.

"I'll think about it," is what I told him.

"Should I tell Brooks you said that?"

"I thought you told him you didn't know where I was," I said. We talked some more and then he reminded me I had called collect and Kimmie would have a fit when she saw the bill.

"Keep in touch, bro."

"Sure," I said. "Don't tell Brooks you know where I am."

That night after work I asked Sugar if she wanted to come over for a while but she said no, her husband was on one of his righteous kicks where he was laying off the sauce. She said he'd be home watching TV and if she didn't show up on time he'd come looking for her. You don't want him to find us, she said. He's a cop and if he found me with some guy he'd kill us both and it'd be legal. This was the first I knew her husband was a cop and I wasn't crazy about hearing that. He'll kill you for sure, she said, going on, and you could tell she enjoyed saying this kind of stuff, liked to watch my reaction...and he'll come up with a story that you were trying to rape me. I guess you'd go along with the story, I said. I guess, she said, smiling this smile you could tell was patronizing, like I was too dumb to believe. Your sidewalk don't go all the way to the curb does it? she said. That a Yankee thing? and somebody, another waitress walking by, heard her and laughed. Suzie was the other waitress. Everybody called her Susie Q, but that wasn't her middle initial or the first letter of her last name. I seen her time card and it said Susan P. Brovard. Susie Q was just her nickname.

She came back out of the dining room and into the kitchen where Sugar and I were still standing there talking.

"Hey, Jake, y'all got nothing else to do you can come with me," she said. I was surprised. Susie Q had hardly looked at me, all the days I'd been working there. I knew she was friendly with a guy I think was named Bruce something, came in every night and sat at the bar and just stared at her. Every once in a while during her rounds to tables, she'd pass by and they'd talk for a minute, give each other the tongue when the boss wasn't around. He always waited until she was done and then she left with him t'suck the corn off his cob, I figured.

"What about Bruce?" I asked.

"History," she said. "Ancient history. Besides, I just asked you to come along. I didn't say I was gonna fuck you, did I?"

Not in so many words, I almost started to say, but held my tongue. Where we went after cleanup was done was this black after-hours place called the Green Onion. She had to wait for me while I prepped the bar for the next day, but she didn't seem to mind. Sat at the bar eating cherries as fast as I could replace them.

We went in her car, one of those death-trap Pintos, down to the south end of town.

"This used to be called Niggertown," she said. "Before integration."

"What do they call it now?" I asked.

"Niggertown."

We were the only white people there when we walked in, but she said I'd be all right since I was with her. Some guy, about the blackest dude I ever saw, and he was dressed all in black, too, even down to the Big Apple hat he was wearing over his fro, made him look like a Gumby licorice stick, came over to where we were at the bar and she introduced him as Slick. Slick wasn't too crazy about white guys, you could tell, but he stuck out his hand and I shook it. Then he promptly ignored me, didn't say another word to me the whole time until him and Susie walked out to the dance floor. That was fine with me. As soon as he and Susie got up to dance, doing some kind of slow strip tease on the dance floor together, this girl came up and sat on Susie's stool.

"I'll take a gin," she said to me. "My name's Saundra."

She was cute, looked like a young Dionne Warwick with less of a Dick Tracy chin.

"Gin and what?" I said, motioning for the bartender.

"Gin and gin," she laughed and flipped around on the stool back and forth, her short skirt flaring up so I could see her legs. They were fine, fine legs.

We had few and talked—flirted, actually—and I was just about comfortable enough to hit on her when someone shoved me in the back, would've knocked me off my stool if I hadn't grabbed the one in front of me, the one Saundra was sitting on.

It wasn't me this guy was shoving. As quick as I snapped around I saw that. *He* had been pushed into me by a much bigger guy. All in the space of a second or two, the smaller guy was shoved into me, the noise died down, the big man said something like *punk* or something to the little guy and the little guy hit him in the chops. Only he didn't just hit him. None of us, including the guy who'd been hit, realized what had happened at first. Not until he put his hand up to his face where he'd been popped, and his fingers slid inside his mouth. My eyes went from the fingers disappearing inside his face to the other guy's hand, and as soon as I saw the flash, I figured out what had happened. He'd hit him with a straight-edge razor.

"Let's book, white boy. This is not the place for you."

It was Saundra, and she was pulling my sleeve. I just nodded and slipped off the stool, only not before I scooped up my change from the bar. We were out in a parking lot before the noise even started up again and shooting down some dirt road before I had time to think.

"Thanks," I said, soon as my head cleared. "Where we going?"

"Here," she said, and pulled off to the side of the road. We were outside of town somewhere, who knows how the hell far from my motel.

"Bye," she said.

"Bye?"

"Did I stutter?"

"You kicking me out?"

She grinned.

"No. I'm *letting* you out."

"I don't get it."

"What—you think I was going to take you home, introduce you to my daddy?"

That wasn't what I thought she was going to do but this wasn't either.

She dropped the grin. "I did you a favor. You'da stayed around that bar you'd be dead right about now. I just got you out. That's it. Period."

"I thought—"

She gave kind of a snort and looked away, out her window. "You thought I was gonna give you some lovin'. Well, I'm not. I've got a boyfriend wouldn't appreciate that very much. Just get out."

I opened the door and swung my legs out. "You could at least take me home, couldn't you? Where the hell are we anyway?"

The corners of her mouth turned up in a smirk. "No I couldn't, Yankee boy. I get seen lettin' you off and somebody

I know sees me I might as well move to New York. We're about a mile from town. Just follow your nose."

"Your friends are prejudiced?"

She laughed then and let her foot off the clutch and the car started to move forward slowly. I jumped out, half falling.

"Say 'thank-you,'" she said, pulling away.

I said something else but I don't think she heard me.

ELEVEN

A little more than halfway to Indiana the Ford broke down, threw *two* rods, which was my fault as I knew it liked oil and I hadn't been feeding it enough. I got thirty bucks for it from a junkyard, caught a bus out of Paducah, and hit the Fort about three-thirty in the morning, which is a good time to arrive at a bus station—no hookers or winos bothering you. I copped a few zees on a bench and bright and early the next day called Mr. Brooks, my P.O., and sure enough, it was like Bud said. Mr. Brooks came down and chewed my ass out, which I had to sit there in his car and take; that was fine, it was what I deserved, but he was a stand-up guy, held up his part of the bargain and drove me over to the halfway house himself. Going in I seen three-four guys I knew from Pendleton and sometimes at the city lockup, and I knew things were going to be all right.

I wasn't in the halfway house a month when Mr. Brooks let me leave. There's lots of stories, mostly bad, about P.O.'s, but I drew a decent one. Your P.O.'s God, believe me, and you get a good one like I did, well…!

Brooks got me a job over at Danny's Tonsorial Emporium, which wasn't nothing but a fancy name for a barber shop that did some styling. Same kind of work as everywhere else, but we shampooed the hair before we cut it and then we blow-dried it. Triple the price. "You make your money on the shampoo," Danny said. "Give 'em a good one." Danny also had the biggest gambling operation in town. I don't know if Mr. Brooks knew that or not, but I don't know as how he could of missed it. We had six phones in the back room was used for nothing but taking and laying off bets.

I always liked to gamble but at Danny's I sort of went wild. It got to the point where I was betting upwards of ten grand a week. Some weeks double that. That was kind of risky being as I was knocking down maybe four hundred in salary on the busy weeks. Except I wasn't losing or winning that much; that was just what changed hands. Like on Sunday I'd start out with five hundred on five-six football games, and maybe I'd come out a few hundred ahead or so, and then I'd do the same on Monday, on basketball, plus a couple on the Monday Night Game in football. Tuesday the same thing. Wednesday and so on. End of the week, I might be up three-four hundred or down the same, even though the total I'd've bet was five figures. More than once, I ended up with a good score, maybe two-three thousand on the week. One week, I hit for almost six thousand. One thing. I never once lost on football overall but basketball was a killer. Too many games, too many teams to follow smart.

Football was different. Especially college football. Danny taught me how to bet smart.

The way he did it, the way he taught me, was to pick out four or five really obscure teams. Slippery Rock University, places like that. Follow those teams, know everything there is to know about them. Danny'd get the town newspaper, the college paper, everything he could get that might have an article or something on the local team. He knew when their left guard was gonna take a shit.

"The way it is," he explained. "There's a guy in Vegas what sets the spread for the whole country. Same guy's been doing it for years and years."

We had a lot of opportunities to "middle" bets. That's

where the smart money was. Middling was hard to do if you were an average schmuck but being as we had access to bookies all over the country it was a piece of cake. Danny was in with the local goombas and they let him lay off money just like he was connected.

Most people don't understand professional gambling. They think bookies want everybody to lose. Bookies thought like that, they'd be out of business in a week. What they want is the money on a particular game to come out fifty-fifty. You got Notre Dame vs. Southern Cal, for instance; you want a hundred grand on N.D. and a hundred going on U.S.C. The bookie don't care who wins or loses—he makes all his money on the juice, the ten percent vig the loser pays. It's a business, pure and simple. A true gambler never gambles—that's a sucker's game. That's for the chumps out in the tool room at Bendix Automotive, guys that drive bread trucks, amateurs like that.

That's why the point spread goes up and down all the time until time for the kickoff. The rule of thumb is, for every twenty-five hundred bucks bet on one team over the other, the bookie jacks up the spread a half point to entice money to go the other way and even it up. If the bookie can't get it even before game time he calls Vegas and lays off the extra.

It's like this: Say Notre Dame plays Alabama in the Sugar Bowl. Naturally, most of the money bet in South Bend and Fort Wayne and Gary is going to be on the Irish and the same thing is happening down in Birmingham and Selma, only the money is going to be on the Tide down there. Bookies in both places get overloaded so they call Vegas and swap money until it comes out even. This is going on all over the country. Ma Bell makes a killing. Ma Bell loves gamblers to death.

What this does is create an opportunity to play the middle. You can't lose on a middle. A middle is when you take advantage of a shift in the point spread.

Say it's the Monday before that N.D.-Alabama game. The Fighting Irish are favored by seven. You bet five hundred on Alabama, get the points. By Friday the spread has shifted to where N.D. is only favored by three. That means you've got a four-point spread to middle. Now you get five hundred down on Notre Dame. The most you can lose is the juice on the loser, fifty bucks. But...if Notre Dame wins by, say, four points, you win both ways. You win the five you bet on Alabama when you had seven points and you win the five on N.D. where you were only giving up three. You win a thousand and all that was at risk was fifty bucks.

There was a time when that's all the smart money did, bet middles. But they fucked up. They let too many of their friends in on a good thing and the bookies shut it down, quit giving the spread out early. Most of them wouldn't release the point spread until just before game time so there wasn't enough time to develop a good middle.

Us guys at Danny's could still do it, though, as Danny had bookies all over the country he was connected with, had different spreads than the ones we had locally. Everybody knew what was going on. The bookies knew and Vegas knew but as long as only a few people were making middle bets they looked the other way. It was kind of a bonus check for bookies and a few of their friends. If they started to abuse it, Vegas would figure out a way to stop it, so everybody tried to be cool.

I was doing pretty good, winning most weeks, and then I took a hit. A big hit. Over six grand. There was no way I could make it up, even middling. Not in time. It wasn't like they were going to break my legs or anything. That's mostly in the movies and not for a measly six thousand dollars. For six thousand dollars they might threaten you if they thought you were the kind ran scared, but guys like me they did something worse to. They just wouldn't take any more bets. They'd write the loss off but I couldn't bet any more.

I'd rather they break my leg and call it even, let me get back in the action.

Only way I could get back in the game was pay them off, and the only way I knew to come up with that kind of money was to steal it. No problem—I figured after a good Saturday night, Smiley's had at least that much for the deposit. Chances were fifty-fifty Smiley would just hide it in the bar until Monday, especially since I knew he had a broad on the side, kept her in an apartment over by Snider High School and liked to take her up to Chicago once in a while on Sundays to watch the Bears game. The times he planned on going to the Windy, I guess he wanted some serious money to impress her with, take her down on Rush Street, wine and dine her to the max after the game. All I had to do was sit around the bar, see if his little girlfriend was there, and if they were lovin' it up, figure he would just leave the money there overnight, pick it up on their way to Chicago next day. No way he'd deposit it if he needed it, and no way he'd take it home so his wife might find it, figure out what he was doing with his bimbo.

That was my plan.

I finally run into Donna, day before I robbed Smiley's. I was down at Alexander's over on State, came in for the take-out ribs, and I turned around and there she was, big as shit, tits hanging half out her blouse and looking like sex with All Caps. It was about three months after I got back. I didn't know what to expect, it being sudden like that, and a surprise, this not being a place where we'd ever gone together, so I wasn't on my guard but you know what? I didn't feel anything. Not a goddamned thing.

That was something, that.

I can't say this hadn't crossed my mind, about running into her. Shit, it was the reason I'd really come back, but I'd just kept putting off looking her up. Once or twice I even dialed her number but I always hung up before she answered. Maybe I thought a guy might answer and I didn't know how I'd handle that.

"Hi, Jake," she said and I could tell she was trying to figure out how I'd react to this, knowing we'd had our violent times, and that felt pretty good, knowing she was up on her toes so to speak, but all I said, and this I couldn't fucking believe, all the speeches I'd rehearsed, even the way my eyes would be, *frosty,* was—"You owe me a new razor cord, sugar."

We stood there a few minutes, toe to toe, just looking at each other, her folding and unfolding her hands down in front of her, her eyes big and wide and...and *bright...glittery*-bright, and I tried to think of something else to say, come out on top, she must think I'm crazy what I just said, not knowing the circumstances, but it wasn't worth the effort; *it just didn't matter.*

Fuck. I did the only thing I could do at that point. I walked past her, just barely brushing her shoulder and went on out the door of Alexander's and out into the cold. It was January and snowing, and there was gray slush on top of the clean snow, the snow plows having just been by, flinging crap all over everything, the sidewalk, all over my windshield, this piece of junk I'd just bought for fifty bucks, another Ford. I didn't have a scraper so I just used the Styrofoam box my ribs were in, trying not to spill them, but got the fries and the French bread and ribs all mixed up, sauce on everything.

Back in my room I kept getting this picture of Donna and

the way she kept folding and unfolding her hands, and right behind it I got this image of Bud and the guy in Tennessee, the one whose hand he squooze and broke and that we left holding his goodies, wishing he had a fig leaf. The whole time she was doing that with her hands, it was like she was doing it to my insides, same as Bud did to that big hillbilly.

Way it turned out, I got shot in the leg breaking into Smiley's over on Vance Avenue, and now here I sit in city lockup awaiting transport back to Pendleton. There was a lot of boozy nights and days, I suppose, led up to me making that kind of mistake.

I usually don't go for the sauce that much and I hate guys who blame everybody but who they ought to blame which is themselves when they lose control, take up drugs, booze, whatever, and so I got to do the same. But all I know is I kept thinking of that fucking bitch Donna. I'm not saying it's her fault—I'm not saying that—fuck, I'm a big boy and ought to be able to keep it cool. I'm not even that sorry I lost it there for a while and I'll be damned if I even knew how it happened. I'm sitting in a bar one day, tossing back a quick one and just about ready to leave, when I thought, what the hell, and I had another one and ended up spending the rest of the afternoon when I should have gone back to work. That was pretty much it for work. It was that second drink did it. Just like that. That's when I started making bets that weren't too bright.

I did a lot of thinking during that period, which is what you do when you drink. Unless you got a compadre wants to sit around getting stinking with you, which don't happen as a rule, all you got to do is think. Think and drink.

It's funny. I've read as much as anybody about why guys like me end up spending half their life behind bars and they've got all kinds of theories except for the right one. Doing crimes is like drinking. It's the same, exact thing.

There's a jolt you get when a job goes down. Ain't nothing like it in the entire universe. Better than whiskey, better than coke, matter of fact, it's better than sex in a lot of ways. I sure never got as high after a mattress marathon as I have after I stick up a guy. That sex high when you come lasts about ten seconds but the buzz you get when you just got off some motherfucker's poke can go on for weeks. It's a drug is all it is. The body's own natural drug. Adrenaline. I finally figured it out and that's the secret. Which means nothing's gonna change in society. Only way it's gonna change is take out the gland makes the adrenaline. It ain't even about money only you couldn't convince the do-gooders of that. They got this idea that if everybody gets a big piece of the pie then crime will disappear. They just don't get it—it's not about money or any of those things.

Besides that jolt, there's one other reason guys pull crimes. For control. Most of us haven't ever been in charge of even a little bit of our lives. Holding a .45 on some clown in a liquor stores makes you God, at least for a few minutes. In the back of your head, you know that situation's gonna come to a crashing halt eventually, but for a few minutes you get to be in charge, make the other guy feel the fear you carried around with you all the live-long day.

When I was pulling jobs, when I first started doing burglaries, stuff like that, I had all the money I ever wanted. Give me twenty bucks, I'd say to my mom and she'd fork over thirty. Any time I wanted. Money wasn't why I broke into places. I did it for the high. All the money in the world, all the things that all the money in the world could buy legitimately for you couldn't duplicate that high. Nothing there is can match that 'cept you pull the crime. If you had a million dollars in your back pocket and you got the crime monkey on your back then you'd hold up somebody for his thumbs, for the lint in his pocket. Whatever. Like they always say about guys who wheel and deal on Wall Street—money's just a way of keeping score. That's all it is and until the sociologists and other book freaks figure that out, there ain't no way criminals are going to disappear.

Once you've had a rush like that it's only a matter of time before you get around to it again. We're like alkies or dopers, us thieves. Same for other kinds of outlaws 'cept maybe rape, but I'm not even sure about that since that doesn't happen to be a trick in my own bag.

You got to get away from anything that makes it easy for you to take up the habit again, get a fix. The Man kind of knows that. That's why they have all these rules when you make parole, like no drinking, no drugs, can't associate with known criminals or other paroles, stuff like that. They know that even if you got the best intentions in the world, you get with other guys who've got the habit same as you, sooner or later one of you is going to get an idea and before you know it, you're out there with a cut-down twelve gauge in your mitts, looking over the counter at the local 7-Eleven at some punk who's stuffing money into a paper bag. It's like being a smoker. You can break the habit for a while, but if you hang out with enough smokers one of these days you're gonna reach over and pick up a butt and then you're smoking again. That's exactly how it happens.

The thing is...there just ain't nothing on earth like crime. Slashing and ripping and tearing up, that's a kick can't be had anywhere else. There was nights when I was going good, had the juice going, when I'd rip off eight, nine, ten places in a row. Not even plan none of them. Just do it. I'm God in a getaway car.

I'd be driving around town, see a bar all dark, and it just drew me in. Park the car a block away, hike on over, check out the layout. No tools, nothing but my smarts. There's those think burglars have all these fancy-schmantzy burglar tools, and sure—there's some do, I have myself, but usually it's nothing that complicated. Most places have glass some-place and wherever there's glass you can get in with nothing more than a rock or a brick. Get in, get out.

Even if there's no glass, at least none you can break through easily, you can go through almost anything. I seen businesses where they had all the fancy locks in the world on their back doors but the wall itself was basically wallboard, something thin like that. A five-pound sledge and a crowbar will take something like that down in two minutes. It always made me laugh I seen a setup like that. They must figure burglars can only go through doors or windows. Hell, if the wall's thin, that's the best place to break through at.

I went in a house once, had these big heavy-duty sliding glass doors on the back. I knew the owners were gone, and it was out in the country so nobody could hear me break the glass. Once I was inside, I had to admire the locks on that door. Nice ones, must have cost a lot of money. The owner even had a steel bar he'd put down at the bottom of the runner. Guy like that must think people who break into houses can't figure out any other way than to pick a lock to get in. Picking locks only eats up time and gets you caught. Bust the fucker down—that's the ticket.

The bolder you are, the less likely you'll get caught. One time, over in Bremen, this little town south of South Bend, I pulled into this strip center had about seven businesses in it, along about two in the morning. Everything was closed up except an all-night Laundromat. Just across the street was a gas station and there were two state police cars parked by the pumps, and both the guys were standing outside their cars jawing, probably about what master criminal-catchers they were. I give 'em a little wave, which they gave back, and went into the Laundromat. In the back was a coin changer bolted by two steel bands to the wall. I went back out to the car, got a crowbar and hammer, and went back in and ripped the machine off the wall. Made all kinds of racket. I carried it out and put it in my trunk, climbed behind the wheel and drove off. On the way by the cops I give 'em another wave and they waved right back. Being bold's the only way to fly.

That was a serious rush. You get a rush like that no way you're gonna be happy sitting home watching "I Love Lucy" reruns. No, you got to have more.

They figure out something a guy can do that will replace that kind of high that's legitimate, they can start tearing down prisons. Ain't likely that's gonna happen. Put too many lazy fuckers out of work. What would cops and hacks and judges have to do? Get a real job? Coffee shops would all close up and doughnut factories would start laying off. You got a whole entire economy depends on criminals.

I've got to come back in three months to stand trial for the thing at Smiley's but first I had to go on back to Pendleton, begin serving the rest of my other sentence, the one I was on parole for. Brooks came down to see me but didn't say much, just kept shaking his head till I let him off the hook, told him it wasn't his fault, there was just some folks are gonna always be in the joint and that I was one of them. Nothing you can do about it pardner, I told him, and when he left we were still friends. He even left me a carton of butts. Show me another P.O.'d do that.

Vance has always been a bad-luck street for me. I got my nose broke in this same bar—probably why I hit it—Smiley's—and my teeth rearranged in the same circumstance. Smiley's changed my smile that time and now Smiley's has changed the way I walk, least till it heals. The bullet went clear through and I found out something. Getting shot in real life isn't anything like you see on TV. On TV, those guys get up after they been hit and keep on doing whatever it was they were doing before, smacking the bad guy, running over the tops of buildings, whatever. Bullshit.

When I got hit I just laid there and bawled like a baby. I admit it. I ain't ashamed of it. I thought I was dying it hurt so bad. I couldn't have walked on that leg any more than I could have flown the first spaceship to Mars. The cops didn't even have to work hard to find me. Just follow the screams to the back room where I'd crawled. I had this idea that if I tried to get up and make it out of there I'd bleed to death, push the blood out faster, something like that. The way my heart was thumping, I figured I'd have all my juice pumped out in about three minutes flat.

Smiley himself popped me. He was laying up on a rafter like he was making love to it, his .22 rifle in his hands. Later, I find out somebody snitched and he knew all along his place was going to get hit that night. Teach you to talk about a job in a booze-joint. It's for sure you never know who your friends are.

Fuck it is what I thought, once the paramed tells me I'm going to be all right. I wasn't even that upset about being caught. You can't do the time, don't do the crime is the motto of every man Jack's ever been behind bars and it was a motto I held to in heart and head. Sooner or later they're gonna get you is what I figured and it was just my time again. It's funny—once I got shot and busted I didn't even much care about the gambling. It's like that happening cured the bug.

What got me in long-range trouble was getting shot. Not getting caught—that's not the trouble I mean. The trouble I'm talking about is the trouble I got into with a black prisoner while I was in lockup waiting for the bus that was going to take me back to Pendleton. The guard said they wouldn't send a bus until they had at least five prisoners and they only had three. Me and two black guys who got popped trying to get rich at an ATM. Frick and Frack. That's what I called 'em. Little Raisenet and Big Raisenet. The gal they pulled a knife on happened to have a gun on her and she even said that old joke when she pulled it out, I heard. "Don't bring a knife to a gunfight, bozos." The black guys didn't tell me that, one of the guards did. Barry. That was the guard's name. Nice guy. We both got a laugh out of that.

None of us knew how long it'd be before they drove us down to the joint. There was another guy who'd already had his trial and was having the presentence investigation being done. He wasn't in with us, was out on bail working at this straight job, hoping the judge would see this and be lenient with him. No way, Barry said; I was this guy I'd have my nose up as much pussy as I could or I'd be on a bus smoking south. He's headed for a fall. Judge Donegal don't cut no repeater loose, Barry said; his lawyer just don't want this turkey to run until he gets paid. Soon as the guy turns his paycheck over to him the lawyer's gonna call Donegal and the presentence investigation is gonna be over. Probably to-morrow bein's it's Friday. You'll be heading back first thing Monday-Tuesday morning.

"You're right," I said to Barry. "Lawyers are all assholes. They got you by the short hairs. Fuckers all sit around the country club with their hands on each other's dicks and then get in court and scream at each other like they hate their guts. Everybody knows it's a scam, but we all put up with it, buy into the deal. Hell, you got to. What else you gonna do? It isn't like you can go get somebody that's going to be square with you. Lawyers, judges, prostitutes, what's the dif-ference?"

Barry just nodded. He was a righteous guy.

Like when I was out on bail for the first bust and pulling

jobs right off the bat as if I hadn't never even hit a speed-bump, when I got popped again. The thing at the motel with the dog. My lawyer from the first time came up and saw me, got them to take me over and sew up my back and he said it was kinda bad, getting arrested while out on bond, but he thought he could handle it. It'd take another grand, maybe fifteen hundred, but he could pull it off most likely.

One of the guards, guy I thought was a righteous dude named Robin something, told me the lawyer I was using was a dirtbag, couldn't get the Pope off for a parking ticket, but he knew this public defender named Brockman was the best legal eagle outside of F. Lee Bailey, and I wouldn't even have to pay the guy, just plead poverty and the court would assign him if I asked.

I bought it, the whole deal—what'd I know?—and fired my lawyer, Mr. Connors, and sure enough, it worked just the way Robin said. I told the judge I was broke and wanted a public defender and could I please have Mr. Brockman, and the judge smiled and said, why not, that's fine with me, only it's on record you paid Mr. Connors so I'm not buying this poor routine, you'll have to pay Mr. Brockman you want to use him.

A month later, I'm sitting in quarantine at Pendleton and a couple of inmates let me know how stupid I was. It seems Brockman *used* to be a fair lawyer but he'd spent all his time these last few years trying to break the land speed record for getting to the bottom of a bottle and had lost his job and family and everything, and the only work he could get was what was doled out to him as a public defender. Robin Jones, that was the name of the guard at the lockup, who was Brockman's shill. Sent him customers and Brockman took care of him. The guy I fired, Connors, was a for-real attorney, won about eighty percent of his cases, which was about the opposite percentage for Brockman.

I ended up paying Brockman the same as I would have paid Connors and the mistake I made was paying him up front. If I'd slow-walked him or told him he wasn't getting his fee until I got cut loose, I most likely wouldn't've ever seen Pendleton. As soon as the check cleared—I had to ask Mom for the money for which I'll be forever sorry—Brockman says the best thing to do is forget this not guilty plea crap and plead guilty—waive my right to a jury trial and take a bench trial, and he'd get it assigned to this judge who owed him a favor. Just plead guilty and I'd be back on the street in no time at all, he said.

You don't never pay your attorney up front, an old con told me. They don't have to do no work then and most of them won't.

Only problem with that advice was that I didn't get it until I was back in Pendleton. Timing is everything in life.

"Your Honor," says Brockman, and that's the only words he got out without slurring his speech. He was dead drunk, but did that matter to the judge?

"My client..." and here he had to look down at the papers in front of him to remember my name. "Mr. Mayes wants to plead guilty but also wants the court to know he's truly contrite over his actions and will never commit another crime as long as he lives if you will but grant mercy in this in-stance."

Whoop-de-do. Some long-winded, flowery speech. I sat there and groaned aloud, at which both the judge *and* my legal eagle both gave me the eye.

The judge was this little ol' baldy peckerwood looked like he was about three sheets to the wind himself, and he looks up over the edge of his throne and said, "Mr. Mayes, your words are handsome but I look at your record and all I see is an incorrigible criminal. Two-to-five, including time already served. Next case."

The whole shebang must have lasted all of six minutes. Last I saw of my lawyer, he was walking at a fast clip out the door. On his way to a meeting with Jack Daniels I figured, way he was stepping smartly, his cheeks twitching. You live and learn.

Anyway, in my present situation, that made four ready to be sent down, and Barry said there was a warrant out on somebody else for parole violation and his cop buddies knew where the guy was, they were trying to decide who would be the unlucky stiff who'd go bring him in. The guy was a head, always high on skag or something and he liked guns. The dangerous ones nobody likes to have to pick up, Barry said, and that made sense. No way I'd ever be a cop. Too many assholes out there anymore putting shit in their veins, thought they was Superfly, The Green Hornet. Some of these clowns, a bazooka wouldn't bring down, only make them crazier. I done dope, who hasn't? But I never let it get to me like some of those weak mothers.

He'd be coming in tomorrow morning, Barry said. Barry was always pulling me out of the cage to mop the floors downstairs, give me a break from the drunks and other derelicts in the tank where they kept all of us. We did more talking than I did mopping. Some of the guards are all right, guys like him.

We're sitting there having a smoke and Barry said the captain has put the word out—get this creep in jail before the weekend. I want good statistics this week, he said, so some-body was going to have to go and roust this bird before the second shift on Friday came on so his bust would go on this week's sheet, and the captain could tell the mayor that he was doing his job and that he could let another week go by without threatening to fire him or demote him to turnkey status. That would be like the chief of surgery being ordered to fetch bedpans, Barry said. There's more than one of us would like to see *that*, he laughed.

My leg was on fire that night when I laid down. I couldn't even sit up and play in the pinochle game like I usually do, but instead hit the rack early, not that it helped, laying down.

Laying there on my bunk when the card games broke up and the bullpen quieted down, everybody hitting the rack, it started to hit me that I was going back to the joint and I thought about what that would mean.

Survival is what it meant.

The main thing was to maintain a low profile. You get nowhere but noticed and dead or hurt in a significant manner if you walk around like some kind of bad ass. Fucking up bad asses or those who think they're bad is what makes reps and reps are what lots of guys are after. Guys in the joint, some of them, anyway, are doing shitloads of time and they've got egos like anybody else. Like some dudes who are doctors, say, or musicians or whatever, they're out to make a name for themselves. About the only way a guy who thinks like that can be a big shot is to kill somebody. There's just some cons who love to walk around with everybody whispering behind their hands when they go by. Gives them a rush, makes them feel like they're somebody. I guess that's it. Erasing some fucker is not something that appealed to me, even if it made people want to line up for my autograph, but there's plenty in the joint who want exactly that.

You're smart, you try and become invisible. Blend. Into walls, furniture. You walk into the day room, say, you pick a spot along a wall. Never in the middle of the room. Paint a bullseye on your back you do that. Never in a corner where lines of sight converge. Not in the middle, even along a wall. Somewhere between the middle and the corner, up along the wall. By an object. Not in the open. A trash can, something like that, something that can take the focus off of you.

Never make eye contact. That's definitely a big rule to

follow. Never. If you do you keep your gaze flat, unemotional. You don't look away too quickly or hold your gaze too long. A second either way can get you noticed.

You adopt a gunfighter's attitude like in the Westerns. Quiet and controlled, as if you could explode from stillness and wreak devastation. You play-act in your mind, get the mind-set, force your body so it's a top gun's attitude.

Quiet means strength. A loudmouth is a motherfucker who's headed for an I.V. hookup in intensive care, or worse.

When you go into a room the first thing you do is take a photo with your eyes and locate possible weapons. Even with every precaution you can take, some silly mother can still walk up and front you. You want a mop handle or a heavy ashtray, something to use as a weapon, that happens. You assume the worst will happen and be ready.

The main thing is, you always try to disappear.

The times you have to pass by a group of guys who aren't friends, you do it with quiet, controlled force, not enough to appear threatening, but with your eyes slightly averted, or better yet, looking through the men like your mind is elsewhere. Like, you're so confident in your badness and abilities you don't even think to be aware of their potential threat.

You never smile with your eyes. There's a trick of smiling with your mouth only and you better learn how to do that. Only with your lips and never a full smile, only a hint. If possible, with a little bit of a sneer, not enough to antagonize, enough to make someone else believe you don't even know you're sneering—it's just the way life has forced your lip to go.

There's a lot of shit to staying alive. A lot of acting. You better be going for the Oscar every minute you're on camera, which is always. In some ways, the joint is a place where even the good times are bad.

* * *

Along about two in the morning, it happened. I should of seen it coming, but no, not me, I'm so wrapped up in my leg that's killing me I couldn't see an elephant if it was bearing down on my monkey ass.

"Wake up."

I could feel his breath on my cheek. I started to raise up but the feel of the razor blade on my neck forced me to forget that idea.

"That's good, Jim. Now. I want you to swing your legs over and hop down. Easy, white boy."

I knew what was coming, but I didn't want to think about it. I couldn't see him, he was behind me, but I knew it was Little Raisinet.

I did what he said, dropped my pants, didn't talk, all that. All the time, I'm waiting for my break, a split second when he would drop his guard. And I'm thinking about my father. The whole fucking time. Like, what would he'd've done if he got caught in this situation. That was a nobrainer. He wouldn't care if the nigger cut him from ear to ear, he'd have to make a play.

I wasn't my father. I found that out in that moment. My father, I knew, would rather die than have someone do what this guy was going to do to me. Me? I guess I just don't have the guts my father did, the guts I always thought I had. Because I didn't want to die. I'd rather be shamed than die.

All I could feel was that razor blade against my throat. Wouldn't it be something, I remember thinking, if this motherfucker screws me and then decides to cut my throat anyway?

Part of me was somewhere else, logical and detached. Would a little razor blade like that cut deep enough to reach an artery? If I twisted to the side could I escape? If I did, could I still keep this asshole from cutting me and killing me? I considered each possibility as it occurred, all the while he's doing his thing and the longer I hesitated and didn't commit to some kind of action the less chance there was of doing anything at all. It was like being in a football game with the clock winding down and you're out of time-outs and you've got to call a play, you're the quarterback, and you've got to come up with something, save the day, and while you're still thinking about it time runs out.

I hardly felt his dick. It was crazy—I almost laughed. I almost said to him, "Hey, I thought niggers were supposed to be hung. You feel like a Bic lighter." I didn't, of course but isn't that wild? I'm getting nailed—*raped*—why call it anything but what it was, and I'm thinking up funnies. It was all over in a couple of minutes and then he was out of my cell and I just stood there another minute wondering if it had really happened or if I was still asleep, dreaming, and then I went over to my bunk and climbed up and laid down on my stomach. I lay there awhile and then pulled off my pants and underwear and wiped myself with my shorts. I wanted to go out to the bullpen to the sink and wash myself—but all I could think of was that everybody there—in the cells that ringed the bullpen—that everybody had heard what was going on. I was too embarrassed to show my face. I closed my eyes, blanked my mind and tried to sleep. I guess it must have worked because the next thing I knew it was morning and the hack was hollering that our rolls and coffee were here.

Gotta get up some time, I thought, and walked out and got one of the day-old breakfast rolls and a tin cup of coffee, and took it back to my cell.

I just stayed in my cell all morning, and after a while I heard Frick and Frack's voices getting louder and louder where they were playing cards at one of the tables. The louder they talked and the more they laughed, the more I couldn't handle it. The big one wandered over and stuck his head in the door and gave me an exaggerated wink. "I'll be by later tonight, sweet meat," he said and went back to his partner, the one from the night before. They both laughed and I heard a couple of the other prisoners snicker this time.

For some reason, I couldn't work up a mad. It was as if I had given up the right to be angry by allowing myself to be fucked like that. All the time before in the joint, I had thought about what I'd do in a situation like that and never had I imagined it would turn out like it actually did. What felt worse—getting nailed by a punk like that—or the fact that I *let* him do that to me, without any resistance—I don't know, but it was as if all emotion in me had disappeared, like I was dead inside only my body didn't know it yet.

I rolled that around in my head, trying to figure it out, what it meant, and an incredible sadness filled me the more I thought about it. The same exact kind of sadness you feel when someone you love has died.

An article I had read years before popped into my head. This guy was talking about relationships between men and women and he said most people get divorced at the seven-year mark in their marriages. The "seven-year itch" is what he called it. His explanation was that all the cells in your body died and were replaced by new cells every seven years and so what you had was two new people living at the same old address. He was wrong. You become a different person when you got raped or something big like that. It was like a big switch was thrown inside and you became this new person, nothing like the old one. Like maybe one of those Hindus who come back to life in a different body. Somebody had taken over my body, that was it. I died and someone else was born. Pretty soon I'd forget the old me and the new soul in me would go on until it, too, died and moved on. Or was killed.

Something in me clicked. I shoved my feet over the edge of the bunk and jumped down. At the other end of the bullpen I could see a mop bucket and mop. I walked out of my cell and straight to the mop, picked it up and broke off the mop part with my foot against the concrete. I walked down to the other end where Frick and Frack were and they must have been hypnotized, watching me, because they didn't even get up when I came up to them, only sat there laughing.

I didn't go after Frick, the one who'd raped me. Not at first. I swung the mop stick as hard as I could and caught the big one square in the mouth. I came from the right, just like I was hitting a baseball off a tee, like I seen little guys doing it out on playgrounds. I finished my stroke and came back from the other side, got him alongside his head, smacked his ear. I think I was screaming something.

Then, I just got the biggest shit-eating grin. I figured I was going to die and I didn't give a shit. I turned around, jabbed the end of the stick into the smaller one's Adam's apple—he'd gotten up and was sneaking around from my blind side—and it felt better than anything I had ever felt before in my life, better than the best sex I'd ever had. When I rammed the end of my stick into his neck I heard my old high school football coach, teaching us how to tackle. *Drive through his body,* he said. *Pretend there's a point on the other side of him you've got to reach.* I don't know how I didn't kill him right then, hard as I poked that stick, but he just went straight down, his hands at his throat, and blood started coming out of his mouth and he was choking but he was still alive. I drew back and hit him as hard as I could with the mop stick and it broke clean in two and over he went. Looked like the side of his head was caved in. You could see the dent where I'd smacked him, and this time he just lay there quietly, blood dripping out of his mouth onto the floor.

The big one was getting up. I'm six-foot-and-a-half-inch-tall, and this guy had at least four, maybe five, inches on me. I could see half his front teeth were gone and blood was everywhere, but he acted like all he'd gotten was a bee sting maybe, and he was trying to decide whether to get mad or not. Kind of slow on the uptake. Before he could react I hit him again with what was left of my stick, this time up along the other side of his head. I don't know if his ears were ringing or not, but he shook his head like he was hearing something in there.

He took a step toward me and that's when the fear returned. And, lucky for me, that's when the guard walked up to the cage.

"Hey!" he yelled, coming around the corner and seeing what was laid out in front of him. Some of the other guards must have been nearby because in a second there were four or five of them there unlocking the door and rushing in. I didn't see Barry but I wouldn't have since he didn't come on until the second shift.

They put me in solitary, which was fine. About an hour later a guard came up and got me and took me down to the day room, the place they use for visits from your family. There was a guy there, all duded out in a suit, tie, briefcase, the works. I sat where he indicated and he introduced himself, but I forget the name.

"What caused the fight?" he said.

"I'm white and they're black," was my answer.

He didn't like that answer.

"You attacked them for no reason?"

"You got it," I said. "I asked them to shine my shoes and they got offended."

There was some more of this and then the guard came and took me back to solitary.

The next day they took me on down to Pendleton in one of the blue busses they use for transporting prisoners. I was the only one on the bus so they must have relaxed their rule that said they had to have five before they made the trip. I guess I qualified for the deluxe ride by busting Frick and Frack's heads.

I wondered when I'd see my new friends again. They were headed for the same place I was. I thought about that a lot all the way down. I'd have to figure something out. I felt good about one thing, though. Actually, two things. One, I felt like I'd regained some measure of honor. Not a full measure, but some. Two, I was going home. I had family there, in Pendleton, homeboys. I was pretty sure this was the first fall for both those niggers. I hadn't seen them around my first stretch. That gave me an advantage.

I just had to figure out how to use it.

TWELVE

Turning off the highway to Pendleton, we went by a sign alongside the road that said, in big black letters on a yellow background, "Penitentiary Area—Beware Of Hitchhikers."

Coming back to Pendleton wasn't so bad. The same day I got there they were bringing a load in from northern Indiana and one of the guys was Manny Del Rio, a big Mexican I knew back in South Bend. It was his first big bust, even though he'd logged plenty of city jail time, mostly for fighting. Turned out he got sent here for fighting this time, too. Only he fought the wrong guy.

Said he clipped a dude up alongside his head in a bar we all used to hang at, Studebaker's. Hit him so hard the guy ended up in Memorial Hospital for an extended stay, the kind where you need help to use the john and it don't matter how foxy the nurse is—you ain't gonna be hitting on her, way you feel. It wouldn't've been a problem, Manny told me, except this guy was an off-duty cop. What should have been a ninety-day stretch at the state farm turned out getting cranked up to a felony and here he was on a one-to-ten. Like, he was supposed to know the guy was the Man. It didn't matter the guy was all liquored up and had started the beef himself over some bimbo; no, it was the way it always was, cop's word is gold-plated no matter what the truth might happen to be.

I was sorry Manny was in here for some no-account bullshit like that, but glad, too. He was a pal and I needed a pal for when my two friends from the Fort Wayne jail showed up, which would be any day now.

That night just before they turned the main lights out, I looked up at the guy rapping on the bars of my cell with his spoon. It was Larry, my last cellmate.

"Hey, dude," I said, jumping up.

He had a bigger smile than me. "Jake. I told you you'd be back. I just wanted to see if it was true. Guy in I.D. told me your name was on the incoming roster."

"Guess you were right, Larry." Fuck'im. All he wanted to do was gloat. Some people are just natural pricks.

"It's *Wherry*, Jake. Dave *Wherry*."

So fucking what? I never was good with names. I got up, lifted my mattress and dug out a pack of Camels and took them over to him.

"Here, Dave."

He looked at the pack of cigarettes in his hand and then at me and said, "What's this?"

"The day I left you said you bet a pack of butts I'd be back. I'm just paying off my debt. I don't want to die owing a shithead like you anything."

"Oh, man, I was just kidding! Here. I don't want these. We never bet anyway. I was just fuckin' around."

He laid the pack on the crossbar.

I laid down on my bunk, crossed my arms behind my head.

"Whatever."

He looked at me another minute and then shrugged his shoulders and picked up the pack and put it in his shirt pocket.

"Well...thanks. Anything I can get you? Anything you need in here till you get in population?"

Nothing I couldn't get myself. "No thanks."

"Well," he said, like he didn't know what else to say. "Welcome back." He stood there like he expected me to say something.

"Whatever."

He turned and left.

There's all kinds of guys like that Dave. Me, I woulda been happy for him he was the one got cut loose, but guys like that can't ever seem to be happy unless they can find someone they think has more misery than they do.

Two days later, coming back from chow, I saw him. Frick. They were bringing him into quarantine, same row of cells I was on, third tier. I was close to the far end by the outside windows and the hack was opening a cell on the opposite end where we come up the stairs. He must have been right behind me.

I ducked into my cell but it was too late. He saw me.

He was bandaged up pretty good, which made my day, but I could feel the fear in the pit of my stomach, which ruined it. When they let us out for recreation I caught Manny, who was two cells down from me, and yanked him back into his cell.

"Manny, I got a problem," I said. I wasn't about to tell him everything. "There's a bro just come in that wants to fuck with me."

"Just point him out," is all he said. That's the way it is in here. You got a friend, you got a *friend*. None of that fair weather bullshit like on the outside. He didn't ask me anything else about the guy only what cell was he in and what did he look like.

"You can't miss him," I said. "He's got bandages all over his head, around his throat. I think he's got a problem with his Adam's apple."

Manny gave me a funny look but didn't say a word.

We stayed in his cell during the rec period. There wasn't much you could do while you were in quarantine. Watch TV, play cards, walk around, maybe cop some dope. Once we got released into the population, there was the gym and the baseball field, weights, horseshoes, activities like that, but in quarantine there was an old black and white TV on one side of the cellhouse and that was it. I hadn't been back long enough to want to stare at the tube yet—things like that I stayed away from as long as possible until I got bored with everything else. That way I always had something in the back of my mind to look forward to. Save it for when my mind was turning to mush. Manny hadn't been in before but he wasn't much for TV anyway, he said.

We talked, shot the shit, made a connection. It happens quicker on the inside than it does out on the bricks. There's no bullshit to get over, trick each other with. We all know why we're here so there's no need to put up a front. All of us are wearing blue dungarees with a number over the shirt pocket and black state shoes.

I told Manny some of the things were gonna happen to him, what to watch out for and who.

"There's one calls herself Alice," I said. "She's a big nigger, almost seven-foot-tall and about that wide. You can't miss her. She's a mean sissy, has this favorite trick of hers." He got interested in hearing this. "She likes to wait until we're coming out of the movie on Saturday morning. There's a place where there's a bunch of bushes just before we hit the quad and that's where you want to watch out. Alice picks out her meat in the movie and then tries to be just in front of the guy right before they walk by those bushes. You'll see guys hurrying to get around her when we come out. Or, laying back."

This was the real deal I was laying on him. Alice was an institution at Pendleton, even the baddest guard wouldn't mess with "her" less he had to.

"What she does," I went on, getting a kick out of watching Manny's face, "is stop sudden-like, like she's digging around to get out her pack of Hoosier and roll one, and then just as the guy she wants walks up, she turns and thumps him on the top of his head. Knocks 'em out, every time. Never heard of her missing. She just picks up the chump and throws him in the bushes and walks over and takes one while everybody's walking by, peekin' over and giggling. Only reason we're giggling is we're just glad she didn't pick on one of us."

"I thought there weren't any women in here?" Manny said, and I wondered what the hell he was talking about, and then I remembered this was his first fall.

"Oh, shit, yeah. I forgot this is your first time. Alice is a guy...well, sort of," I said. "He's a queen, Manny. A faggot. Well, maybe not a complete queen. He's...a whaddya-call-'em, a transvestite. After a while you get to thinking of them as women. They just seem that way to you. You'll see."

"Not me, man. I ain't never gonna see some guy as a chick. I don't care I'm in here a hundred years. And I don't get it. I thought sissies all wanted to suck *your* tool, not the other way around."

"On the outside yeah. It's not like you think in here. This ain't the street."

I never, *never* understood it. In my mind, a guy goes down on another guy or fucks him or has it done to him—it don't matter which—is a fag, but the guys in here, they don't see it like that. They see it as getting over, being a man. Go figure.

And it don't matter if they been inside a day or ten years. It isn't something like they're just so horny they just got to get their trouser worm stroked. Actually, it doesn't have anything to do with sex, I don't think. It's to do with power, who's got the hammer.

I got in this discussion once with this black guy in the barber school who was a righteous dude, didn't fuck with the whites, didn't fuck with anybody, not even his own. Did his own time, kept to himself.

"Yarrow," I said, "how come the brothers don't know that's being queer, fucking white boys?"

"'Cause it's not," he said. "You don't think they'd do it on the outside do you?"

That was true. I'd see the biggest faggots in Pendleton, the daddies with the most kids, black guys, and out on the street I'd run into them and they'd have a babe on their arm. They really didn't see it as a homosexual thing at all.

Manny said, "But why do you call them 'she' or 'her'? They're guys, whatever they call themselves. Doesn't make sense."

I laughed. "Look around, Manny. You see anything makes sense?" I walked over, lifted my mattress, got another pack of butts and came back.

"Fags like Alice, they're different in here, too. Sure, they're uptown ho's, put it out on front street whether they're in here or out, but in here they play a different role. They play the same role the other daddies do. Back out on the street you walk up to them and say 'boo!' they're gonna fall down, actin' like they're some kind of helpless little lamb or something. Don't ask me to explain it. It don't make sense to me either, but it's the way it is."

We talked about some other things. I tried to explain how things were in here so Manny'd know what to do, what to expect.

I remembered the first time I got sent up. I told Manny about it.

"You got it lucky, man. First day I got here they'd had a

riot the day before, busted out all the windows and burned everything there was to burn. They burned the sheets, blankets and pillows, the whole whazoo. The old warden, guy who was here then, was a hardass. He said you burned your shit you can just do without. It was February, man! I got off the bus from South Bend, got deloused and my hair cut, and got my clothes and then they put me in a cell down on the second level, almost right under where we are now. I went to sleep on steel slats—remember, there was no mattresses. They did give us a little bitty Army blanket, didn't even cover my feet it was so short. I woke up the next morning with snow on my toes where it come in the windows that night. About half of us come down with pneumonia and worse, and that bastard still wouldn't give us mattresses or sheets or even fix the windows."

A guy walked in front of Manny's cell and looked in. "You Jake?" he said. Fuck me, I thought; Frick is calling me out already, but then I saw the guy's shirt and knew he was an old-timer by the number stenciled on it—it was older than mine—and I remembered seeing him in the yard from before when I was here. I think he worked over at the auto shop.

"I'm Jake," I said, standing up. "You're Walter, ain'tcha?"

"Yeah," he said, putting his hand out, turning the palm up. There was a piece of paper there. I took it, stuck it in my shirt pocket. "Welcome back, Jake," he said. "Your friends know you're here. I got to get back. The hack only let me in for a minute." Cons in the population weren't allowed in quarantine except if their job took them there. Like the new guys would get contaminated by them or something in the two weeks they spent there before going out in population. Walter was gone before I could say anything. I took out the piece of paper and opened it. All it said was, "Fucked up, didn't you partner? See you in pop." It was signed D.B.

Sonofabitch! It was Dusty! I thought he'd be gone by now, up in Michigan City.

Next morning it happened. We're coming back from chow, same fucking powdered eggs and cold, greasy bacon I'd have to get used to all over again, and coming up the staircase to our cells for the half-hour lockdown and count before we got let out again for the different shit we went through in quarantine: Meet your counselor, get photographed and printed in I.D., take a bunch of tests, crap like that. Put in for your work classification. I was going to put in for the barber school, see if I could get back in.

We're coming up the stairs, Manny and me, and behind us I hear a commotion. I looked back, and sure enough, it was Frick, shoving his way through guys and yelling at me to wait up.

"That's him," I said to Manny. I wasn't scared of him at that moment. There was no way he'd have a shank. It was almost impossible to get a shank in quarantine. We got shook down every five minutes, and every time we left our cells the hacks would be in there, tossing it. Out in the population it was a lot easier to come up with weapons, but here in quarantine, in cellblock H, it was just about impossible the way they kept an eye on us.

I had to give the punk credit. Here I'd already half-killed him and he was going to get in my face. It was 'cause he'd fucked me, was what it was, give him all those guts. He figured he was over, psychologically. Surprised is what he was going to get, I thought. I knew how these cockroaches worked. I was glad he picked quarantine to make his move. Out in the population, later, it would be different. There he'd have a weapon, probably a bunch of his rappies with him, and I'd be up Shit Creek, I didn't watch my step—be careful where I went, what kind of situation I walked into. Here, up on the third tier, it was just me and him, and I had no doubt how that'd turn out.

I could read this little slime like a book. He was gonna come up and break bad, get in my face and start talking about how he was gonna fuck me up. He was the kind had to talk about it first, what a bad ass he was, and that was going to be his mistake. Soon as he got close to me and started running his mouth, I'd pop him. Hit him in the throat, see if I could finish the job. Hit him where he was already tenderized and that'd take all the sand out of him. I was going to break every bone in his body.

I never got the chance.

Just before he reached me, Manny stepped forward and grabbed him, one hand in his nappy hair and the other on the seat of his jeans and flipped him over the side of the railing. It happened so fast, it didn't register for a second. Man! Manny Del Rio wasn't the biggest guy in the world, actually, he was a couple of inches shorter than me, but he was just about as wide as a Maytag. He was one of them body builders, always working out with the bench presses and the wrist curls.

I thought he'd dropped him. From three tiers up. He hadn't though. He just let go of the guy's hair and grabbed him by the ankle and then let go of his jeans. He was holding him by the one leg with his left hand like you'd hold up a rabbit you just shot to show your ma. Frick was crying like a baby. He'd skipped the screaming part it'd happened so quickly. And water was running down his face in a steady stream and it smelled terrible all of a sudden. It took a minute to figure out he was pissing his pants. And shitting. He couldn't even talk, just kept whimpering some kind of mumbo jumbo like a little kid.

Manny held him farther out from the railing, still by one

hand, and it looked like he wasn't even breaking a sweat. I don't think his arm muscle was even flexed. I looked at his face and he had this gentle smile on it, and he leaned over and said, "Punk, I'm having a hard time deciding what to do with you. Do I drop you or do I haul you back up? That's the question that's rambling around in my head. Maybe I ought to ask my friend Jake here what I should do. What do you think?" Fucking Clint Eastwood movie!

Some more baby talk from Frick, nothing you could really understand. The words anyway. I think we both knew what he was trying to get out.

All along the tier I could see guys stopped, watching. Some of them were grinning, the white ones, and others , mostly the black guys, were standing there like they didn't know what they should do, help out the brother or stay the fuck where they were. Since nobody was moving, I guess they decided to stay out of the play. Just then, I seen a hack walk around the corner downstairs and look up. He must have realized what was going on because he just turned around and walked back the way he'd come, disappearing around the corner. He didn't hurry, went back at the same pace he'd come in on. No way he was going to get involved in this business by his lonesome. Smart hack.

"I'm gonna be a nice guy," Manny said in this slow and easy voice. He hauled the guy up and back and laid him sandwiched over the top bar of the railing. Frick grabbed the middle rail and pushed himself the rest of the way over, falling to the walk, and lay there on the concrete curled up like a baby. You could smell the stink.

Manny leaned down close to the guy's face. "You a lucky bro," he said softly. "You fuck with my friend, you fuck with me. You want to keep that in mind, sissy. You understand?"

It had been deathly quiet up till then, although I didn't

notice it until the whole row of guys started babbling and I saw four hacks come around the corner down below. "Time to go in, Manny," I said. All of us along the walk melted into our cells. All except Frick, who just laid there. Somebody, one of the guards, pulled the lever and all the cells swung shut, leaving Frick outside. The four guards came and picked him up, arguing about who was going to have to hold his legs.

They kept us locked up for a good hour longer than usual but nothing ever happened. Usually something like that goes down, we all get questioned, but for some reason they didn't this time. The only thing was, when they let us out for noon chow, the guard who pulled the lever to let us out said to Manny when we walked by, "Good thing you didn't drop that nigger, boy," but he was smiling.

Frick didn't show up the rest of the week and a half. Manny and I were in quarantine, and about a week later, one of the guards I knew from before, Mr. Jones, told us what happened—strolled over to us during recreation one night while we were playing bouree and give us the lowdown. Turns out Frick requested solitary and they gave it to him, and then they let him go out into the population a week early. He was over in J House and had a job in the laundry.

"You're lucky Dobbs was on duty that day," Mr. Jones told Manny. "Dobbs is a KK'er, hates niggers. That been anybody else, you'd be in the hole, half your ribs caved in." It was funny to hear Jones say the word "niggers" being as he was as black as two ayem in solitary his own self. Or to hear him talk about the KKK, like he was a redneck himself.

I was glad Manny'd done what he done but I knew it meant more trouble down the road, this guy had any pride at all. He'd been fronted big-time in front of fifty guys, and the only way he'd ever get his face back, he'd have to kill me and Manny. I told this to Manny, but he was sharp, even though it was his first time in the joint.

"I know that, Jake. I knew that before I made my move. Things here aren't that much different than on the street. Don't worry about it, amigo. That little pissant ain't gonna bother us none. Next time I'll drop him. I think he knows that."

"You better hope he's not a dopehead," I said. "He gets shit in his arm he's gonna think he's Superman again."

"Then I'll kill him," was all he said, like he was talking about the chance of rain tomorrow. Manny was solid.

They put us out into population and we both got our request granted to go to K Dorm and when we got there it was great. Ol' Dusty was waiting for us, sitting on a bunk, had a pile of cigarettes and Oreos next to him.

"For you guys," he said, handing each of us half a dozen packs of cigarettes each and a package of cookies. Manny looked at me, left eyebrow arched and I said, "It's all right, Manny. He's a good guy. Manny, meet Dusty. Dusty's a homeboy."

Dusty had a good gig going and he was gonna cut us in on it. Dusty had become a principal loan shark it turned out.

THIRTEEN

K Dorm was in a two-story cellhouse, up on the second floor, and integration hadn't yet hit Pendleton at that time. One side was all white dudes—Redneck City—and the other side was Little Africa. Below us was regular cells where they kept the perverts. Child-molesters, creeps like that. Some good guys, too, guys that were just too bad to put in a open dorm. Too mean, even for Pendleton. Maybe they killed another inmate, maybe they had been in a riot and the hacks thought they were the ringleaders. Situations like that.

We had all the white weightlifters in our dorm, too. They liked to fuck with the blacks on the other side. Each side was a big open room with two rows of bunkbeds and a couple of big folding tables up at the front by the door for us to play cards on. Same thing over across the hallway in the black dorm. There were two big windows ran the width of the room, barred of course, but where you could look out and see the inmates on the other side. The weightlifters were all nutcases. Most of them hated black guys. I figure that's why they became weightlifters, 'cause they used to be puny and got hit on or maybe even raped like I had when they first came in, and then they lifted weights until they were Charles Atlas. Whatever the reason, I never knew hardly a one of them didn't hate the guys next door. Almost every morning they would all grab sheets from our bunks and throw them over their heads and gather up around the front windows, agitating the guys across the way. Over on their side the blacks would go berserk, scream and yell they was gonna fuck all us up and then when the doors would break open to go to work, not a one of them said a peep, just filed down quietly with us, side by side. I mean, would you want to fuck with guys who could bench-press a Chevy truck?

The dorm was great in a lot of ways. I mean, you had all your buds and the main thing was you had room to walk around, whereas in the cells you were penned up in this little tiny space. The only thing about being in a cell that I missed was your solitude. You never got a minute's peace in the dorms. There was always guys around talking, laughing, shouting, whatever, and there were times you just wanted to be alone. Maybe everybody didn't feel that way, but I did. Lots of times I just wanted to lie down, read a book, but the minute you did somebody would walk over and start jacking their jaw and that was the end of your quiet time. Two of the main things I hated was this, the lack of solitude and the fact there was never a time when it was dark. There were lights on twenty-four hours a day, even at night when you slept. That gets old quick.

Also, going to the bathroom. In the dorm the stools were right out in the open in the shower area. In the cells at least you could take a dump in privacy if you didn't have a cell-mate. Some guys didn't mind and while I'm not especially delicate, there was something about sitting on the crapper in full view of fifty guys walking around scratching their nuts, playing cards, whatever, that didn't make it the most pleasant experience there was. Usually I'd try to wait to shit at barber school where there was at least a concrete half-wall separating you from the rest of the people even though everybody was always yelling, "Did something crawl up and die inside you, Jake?"

And back in the cells you had music. Not the greatest.

Pendleton had one station, run by an old rummy con whose taste ran to what I called "Double-Wide Trailer Park Jams," liked to play the same six songs over and over. There was a wall jack and you got earphones at the commissary to plug into it. I kinda missed that. At night, midnight exactly, a train always ran just outside the walls and tooted its whistle the whole time it was going by. The disc jockey, name of Jake, same as mine, always played the same song when it was going by. Porter Waggoner's "The Green, Green Grass of Home." That, or Bobby Bare's "Detroit City." Like to make you go berserk listening to that lonesome whistle outside the walls, listening to that sad, sad song. That was when guys made a bedsheet necktie, jumped off the bunk in their cells and danced the Last Tango. About once every two-three months all the lights would dim, go out and then kick back on when the emergency generators cut in. Somebody'd taken their illegal hotplate and dropped it in the sink while they were holding on. It always happened in the middle or the end of that song, seemed like.

It's weird but I *liked* that. The song and the train. It was the saddest I've ever felt but it felt good in a twisted kind of way. It was such a deep fucking sad, reached down into your bones, I guess what it was it made you feel alive, more than at any other time. It's like you were on the edge of taking the pipe yourself. Only way I can describe it is you just tried to hold onto the feeling long as possible, milk it for all it was worth just like you try and hold your nut till you're ready to explode when you're having sex. It hurt but it hurt *good*.

Over in K Dorm you could hear that same train, although there were times everybody was still making so much racket it was hard to make out, so it wasn't the same. Once in a while you just need a major league sad to get you straight, let you know you were still a human being, had the same kinds of things going through you as regular people, straights, did.

That time before when I had the toothache from the beans, I remember I'd hear one of those songs and it didn't mean a thing. I didn't feel it. That's when Larry, I mean *Wherry,* started signifying on me. He might have been right. When you can listen to "The Green, Green Grass of Home" in here and not get punky inside, you're a con can do easy time.

I remember hearing that song once in a while on the bricks, and I'd pull over if I could, and just put the car in park and close my eyes and try to get that feeling back. It wasn't the same and I missed it. I don't know if there's a better feeling you can experience than listening to "The Green, Green Grass of Home" and hearing that train whistle while laying in a bunk at Pendleton at midnight, the back of your mind thinking about all the things that were going on back home that you were missing out on and would for a long, long time, maybe forever.

Except for that, K Dorm was the best place to be in Pendleton. Manny and I were lucky to get assigned to it coming out of quarantine. Usually, you had to go to J or one of the other cellhouses and then earn K the old-fashioned way, as they say in that ad. Pay somebody off. They'd tell you it was awarded for good behavior but that was horseshit. Twenty bucks to the hack who was in charge was what got you K. I figured Dusty had something to do with us getting put there and I was right.

"Fuck, man," he said. We're all firing up Camel regulars, sitting on his bunk. "I couldn't let my rappy go into J, could I? You'da done the same for me."

"Man, this tastes good," Manny said, sucking on his cigarette. "How do guys smoke that Hoosier shit?"

We both laughed, Dusty and me. We'd smoked enough of the crap the state gave out free. Hoosier. It wasn't tobacco, no matter what they told us. Wheat chaff is what we called it. Loose bits of brown shit in a white gauze bag with a drawstring. They gave you papers too, crap that came apart if you used too much spit. You ate about as much "tobacco" as you smoked. They claimed it was Indiana tobacco, grown down in the southern part of the state, but I never heard of no tobacco grown in Indiana. That was all done over in Virginia, places like that. Whatever it was, it was nasty stuff, but if you didn't have any green on the books that's what you smoked if you wanted a cigarette.

That was one of the ways the blacks found new meat. They see a guy smoking Hoosier they knew he was poor. Slip the guy a deck of real butts and he was theirs if he took it. Same way they'd watch to see which of the new guys showed up at the chowhall on payday. Guys who had money skipped evening chow that day, filled up on Oreos and other sweet stuff they bought from the commissary. You didn't have any money, you went to chow. It wasn't hard to figure out who might need a daddy, be in the right frame of mind.

I got another break besides getting assigned to K Dorm coming out of quarantine. I got back in the barber school. Manny, too.

Barber school was by far the best lick in the entire joint. It was one of maybe only two or three jobs where you actually learned a marketable skill. There wasn't much call for making license plates on the outside and most of the other gigs weren't much better. Places like the laundry, the metal shop, the chow hall—all they did was prepare you for a low-paying, dead-end job when you got cut loose. Be a fry cook in a greasy diner, work for minimum wage in a dry cleaners. They talked all the time about how good the training was in the metal-working shop but guys who'd been out and come back said they couldn't get a job in a real shop because all the Pendleton equipment was too old and never used anymore in real life.

Barber school was different. Barber shop owners on the outside were waiting in line to get you to work for them. The reason was we were a thousand times better trained than the guys who went to school on the outside.

In "straight" schools students got maybe two or three heads to cut each day. At the Thomas R. White School (the name of Pendleton's barber college) we averaged fifteen heads a day, more than the guys on the outside did in a week. Plus, guys outside only went to school for nine months before they graduated and took their state exam. The least anyone in here was in school was two years, and in most cases at least double that. We were the best haircutters in the state and everybody in the business knew it. At the state exam we blew everybody away. Hardly anybody from Pendleton or Michigan City scored less than ninety-five percent on the test and our practical exams, where you did a haircut and a shave were works of art.

It was a hoot to watch barber students from the outside shave. They'd shake. Their hands would be twitching like they had a disease. I wondered what their models thought when they looked up and saw that razor bearing down on their throats with the guy's hand shimmying like his wheels were out of balance. We gave maybe three-four shaves a day, every day, and most of the guys on the outside were lucky to get in a shave a month. One of our tests in the school was the instructor, Mr. Bowden, would lather up a balloon and we'd have to shave it without popping it. Try that!

When I took my test in Indianapolis to get my license the first time in Pendleton, I didn't have a model for the practical part of the test. That was a common problem for inmates, being as we didn't know anybody on the outside we could get. Most guys' families had given up on them, gone their own ways. Disowned their sons, husbands, whatever. So what we did was Mr. Dillsie would head down to Skid Row in Naptown and try and line up a bunch of bums needed haircuts and shaves, and get 'em over to the place where we all got tested, usually one of the barber schools in Indianapolis. You talk about a smelly bunch! You'd have to shampoo them six times to get half the crud out of their hair.

The guy I ended up getting was in the middle of a severe case of d.t.'s, kept jumping up out of the chair as giant cockroaches or something scary bore down on his alkie ass. I got through the haircut somehow, but when it came time to shave him, that was a different story. He was so far gone with his habit his cheeks were wall-to-wall capillaries. You could touch his skin with the lightest pressure and it'd turn beet red, the skin was so rice-paper thin. No way one of those guys from one of the outside schools could have shaved him without starting a major hemorrhage. They'd have to have the ambulance standing by. I remember whispering to Dusty, who was taking his test at the chair next to me, that I'd probably get my license and get arrested at the same time for killing my model. Especially the way he was twitching.

Didn't even nick him the least little bit, which was good, seeing as how he would've never quit bleeding. The state barber board guy came by and shook his head as I was starting, and when I finished and he came up to inspect, he took me aside and said, "Son, that is as fine a piece of shaving as I've ever seen. I couldn't've done half as well myself and I've been at this thirty years." I scored a perfect score on the written test, as well, and there wasn't a single hair out of place on my haircut. Not bragging, almost all of us from Pendleton done just as well.

There was another benefit to being in barber school. It was a money-maker. If an inmate wanted a good haircut he had to cross your palm with something, at least a couple packs of butts or some green, usually a buck. Otherwise, you fucked him up. The last thing somebody with an upcoming visit from his lady wanted was a chopped up haircut.

So, I'm back in K Dorm and I'm back in barber school and I'm with my old pard Dusty. Things couldn't be better if it wasn't for Frick. Sooner or later, we'd have to get it on. There was no way around it for either of us. One of us would have to die.

I told Dusty about my problem with Frick. I didn't tell him what had happened back in city jail that started it all off, but I think he guessed. It didn't matter—Dusty knew I wasn't any punk and there's no shame in being overpowered—long as you do something about it when you can—but I still wasn't about to tell him the whole story.

"How you want to do it?" was all he asked.

"I don't know yet. When the time comes I might ask for a little help."

What I had in mind was, I would need an alibi in case I was questioned. Long as I had another inmate say I was with him or whatever when Frick bought it, I was in the clear. The warden wouldn't believe me, but as long as I had somebody saying I was someplace else at the time Frick got killed he wouldn't care much, either. It would come down to our word against whoever might snitch me out and being as it would be just some inmate killed another there wouldn't be much fuss over it. Shit like that happened all the time.

That was all that was said about my situation at the time but I felt better. When the time came I would be all set. The thing that scared me was getting my good time fucked up, maybe even catching another sentence. It wasn't that I minded doing extra time—I just hated the thought of doing time for that scumbag.

"I want to talk to you about something else," Dusty said, and he included Manny when he said that. "I got a sweet deal going on." The deal was loansharking. Basic stuff. I loan you five packs of cigarettes for a week and you pay me back a carton. Stuff like that. Dusty wanted Manny and me for muscle. Take care of slow-walkers, deadbeats. Guy slow-walked you, didn't pay up on time, you had to do something. Break his arm, something like that. Deadbeats, they got whacked. Last thing you can have, you're in the loan business, is have somebody not pay up. Guy deadbeats you and the others find out, you're out of business in five minutes. It's a sign of weakness and you can't ever afford to look weak. Look weak for five seconds and you'll be sucking somebody's dick, that's for sure. On the bricks, owing six thousand smackers don't get you squat, but in here, owe somebody a single deck of butts and you can end up rendered room temperature.

I didn't mind breaking an arm or leg or two, but I didn't know about whacking guys. Manny said about the same thing.

"Think it over," was all Dusty said. "It's not as hard as you think and it's not like you have to do it every week. Maybe never. I only had to do it once myself and I been in this business over a year now."

We talked it over, Manny and I, and the more we thought about it, the more we thought we'd do it. Neither of us had anyone who was going to send us money and the thought of smoking Hoosier for the next couple of years was depressing.

"Count us in," we told Dusty the next day. "Whadda we gotta do?"

Nothing, at least for a while, he said. Deliver some shit to people, cookies, cigarettes, stuff like that, to guys who wanted to borrow from him. Green. That was the hinky part. No big deal if a hack caught you with a carton of cigarettes, six bags of cookies. You got caught with green in your possession—that was bad news. Green—real money, greenbacks, were strictly outlawed in the joint. That was because of escapees. Lots of guys escaped—trustees who could go outside the walls—only they mostly got caught quick on account of they didn't have any money to get anywhere. If they had green—real money—they could maybe get on a bus or something before anybody knew they were gone. The state police had a conniption fit then, since they had to actually go out and do their job.

"When we go into the barbershop tomorrow," Dusty said. "Take these with you." He tossed each of us two cartons of Camels. "You'll have two guys come in want these."

How were we supposed to know who they were, we asked.

"They'll know you," he said. "They'll be on your book for haircuts."

"Randy'll have the guys go to your chair," Dusty explained. "I'll give you the sign when they come in." Randy was the inmate who worked as the barbershop receptionist.

Dealing was pretty open. I mean, everybody—guards, instructors, everybody—knew it was going on all the time, but you still didn't want to get caught passing contraband around. Hell, there were at least three hacks were major dealers themselves. We'd have to be careful giving the cigarettes to Dusty's customers but that wouldn't be hard. There was always a guard on duty, and the instructor himself, Mr. Dillsie, would be around, but Randy was going to get a phone call from up front asking the instructor to go up to the officer's barbershop and the hack on duty, Mr. Clifford, went outside about every twenty minutes to have a cigarette. We'd pass the butts then.

Only we never got the chance. Ten minutes before noon a full-fledged riot broke out.

FOURTEEN

Riots were nothing new. I'd been in eight of them last time I did time. Nine, if you count the one I came into when I hit quarantine my first day. That riot was over but I sure suffered through the consequences! Lyndon Johnson was president during my first stretch and he came on the tube one night and said the government had done some kind of study and it was their opinion that Pendleton was the single worst joint in the U.S. We were having a riot a month then, seemed like. When the president made that announcement on TV, every single inmate stood up and cheered like we'd won the championship of the NFL.

This was Manny's first riot but I told him to hang with me and he'd be all right.

"The thing to do," I told him, "is stay out of the way of the crazies. There's guys go nuts, times like these. A guy can get killed just standing around picking his nose the wrong way. Maintain a low profile, that's the key to staying alive."

That was good advice for all the time, not just during a riot. Time after time, I seen guys come in and start breaking bad right from the gitgo. You could tell they was actually scared and that's why they were trying to act like Charles Bronson, but it was the wrong thing to do. You draw too much attention in the joint, your ticket's gonna get punched. Don't matter how big you are or even how bad you might actually be. There's always somebody bigger and badder. Or littler and badder. I found that out myself, didn't I? Somebody got a razor blade to your throat it don't matter if you're eleven feet tall.

If you're smart, you get in the habit of fading into the woodwork. Blend, baby, blend! Anybody stands out, they might as well write *MAJOR DUMBASS* in red crayon on their back. There's too many dudes in here can't wait to establish a reputation and the only thing that impresses a con is taking somebody out, whacking them. You get to loud-talking folks, acting tough, you just put your whole front on the line. You got to keep it up. Really, you got to act badder and badder and sooner or later somebody's going to front you and then you better come through, kill his ass, or it's your own. It's not smart to break bad—not unless you are the baddest dude ever lived, for real. Tough guys in here, *really* tough guys, they see an act like that, they know there's not much else there. Quiet guys, guys that don't say much, keep to themselves, now there's a mystery about them most people don't want to fuck with. They might just be quiet little punks scared to death...or, they might be the nastiest motherfuckers on the block. Nobody knows and nobody wants to especially find out. That old saying about "don't judge a book by the cover"—that got started in a joint somewhere, I'd bet money on it.

There's one thing for sure started in some joint somewhere. High fives. I see guys on the street high- and low-fiving each other and I got to smile. Guys in the joint, old-timers, know where that came from. It came from not trusting any other motherfucker. You meet a guy, you sure as hell aren't going to shake his hand. Do that, put your hand in another guy's hand and all he has to do is yank you toward him, put a shank in your gut. An old-timer told me that at chow one day. He claimed he was doing time in Chino back in the early fifties when they started doing it, couple of white guys who'd had a fight and then decided to bury the hatchet. The brothers saw it, picked it up, and now everybody thinks it started as a black thing. They think it's a *sports* thing!

We were over in the barber school when this riot broke out. The whistle blew and the phone in Mr. Dillsie's office rang at the same time and we all knew some shit was going down, even though when a bunch of us ran to the window we couldn't see anything.

Mr. Dillsie came out, his face as white as an Eskimo's ass, and give the guard on duty the high sign. Jonesy, the guard that day, came running over and they stood together, talking low so nobody could hear them, and then Jonesy says, "Okay, men. There's been some trouble over at the hospital and everybody has to go back to the cells." He started lining us up, barber students on one side, inmates that were there for a haircut on the other. Mr. Dillsie was running around gathering up all the straight razors that had been checked out to put away in the cabinet, which was heavily locked at all times. That was a joke—they had three big Yale locks on the razor cabinet, like that meant something, when three-fourths of the guys in here were B&E guys, could open a Yale in about six seconds flat if they took their time and worked with their eyes closed and were dead drunk, a lot faster if they were on top of their game. I guess the locks made Dillsie feel secure.

They got us back to K Dorm, all of us barber students except one lived there and the one that didn't, a guy we all called Sniffles because his nose was always running. We found out later Sniffles never made it to J Block where he lived; both he and Jonesy got stabbed, him dead and Jonesy cut bad enough to miss three months of work when it was all over. I'da been Jonesy, I wouldn't of come back.

In K we were all right. Looking out the window we could see the riot escalate until there were inmates all over the yard between us and the chow hall. First thing they did was bring down the American flag from the big flagpole out in the center of the yard and replace it with a professional looking Jolly Roger. Some talented seamstress must have sewn it in craft class—it was a beaut. Corny, but it got all of us and we all cheered when we seen it go up, busting with pride like we'd done something major, like win World War Three or something.

"You guys know what this means, don't you?" said Dusty. Me, him and Manny were all clustered at one of the end windows watching the merriment below.

"No food," he said. "Nobody's going to the chow hall until they get this thing shut down."

"What if they don't?" Manny said. "What if this goes on for a week?"

"Then we don't eat for a week."

He was right. The first thing the warden did in a riot was cut off the food supply. They figured if the rioters got hungry enough they'd cave in and go back to their cells. Like they couldn't just go over and take over the chow hall and get their own. That was the first fucking place took over every riot I ever seen. The only ones a shutdown hurt were the ones like us, locked up. We weren't too bad off though. Not with Dusty the loan shark. He had about six weeks worth of Oreos alone, plus potato chips, candy, stuff like that. It'd wipe out his stash, we were on lockdown very long, but the main thing is we weren't about to starve. We might get shanked by our friends for the food but we wouldn't die hungry.

"Fuck!"

"What?" Both Dusty and I both responded to Manny.

"We're gonna miss the movie."

He was right. This was Friday and we always got a movie on Saturday morning. And for once, they had one scheduled that wasn't forty years old and didn't have John Wayne in it. Somehow, in a bureaucratic mix-up, they'd scheduled "Shane" with Alan Ladd. The fact that it was only about twenty years old made it like a sneak preview, compared to the turkeys we usually got.

Right then, something happened that made us forget our disappointment. Smoke. From the chow hall. First, someone yelled "Smoke!" which we could all see plainly, and then fire itself appeared inside the windows. They were burning the tables. And probably anything else combustible they could find, piling it in the dining area and setting it ablaze.

"This is getting serious," Dusty said, and I knew what he meant. Once guys started burning stuff they wouldn't stop. If they got the idea to start on the cellhouses we were in deep doodoo. Below us was one of the worst cellblocks in here and there was no doubt in my mind it'd be one of the next places to go. And we were locked in.

Or so we thought.

"It gets hinky, I can get us out," Dusty said. He said it in a low voice like he didn't want anyone else to hear what he said.

Turns out, Dusty had a key would open the barred door. Bought it for a hundred green years ago from another inmate who'd somehow copped a wax impression from the master key that unlocked all the cells and had a duplicate made up over at the metal shop. Dusty said they changed the locks and the civilian who'd come in to make it had laid it down for a couple of minutes. There were several copies around here and there. Dusty's was the only one in K and nobody knew he had it. Except us. Now.

"Keep your mouths shut," he said, saying it more for Manny's benefit than mine. "I ain't gonna use it unless we start going up in smoke and they don't want to let us out."

The reason he bought it he said, was he always had an

idea in the back of his mind he might make a break sometime. So far, he hadn't figured out just how to bring that off other than to get out of the dorm some night. He was pretty sure he could get past a couple of the front gates with it, as well, but beyond that he wasn't sure. There was no way it'd fit the main door.

Right now the fire seemed to be going pretty good over at the chow hall. There were inmates running around all over the place. Not a single guard was in sight. They must have gotten them all out. So far, nobody, inmate or guard, had come up to K Dorm, let us know what was going on, and everybody had a theory. The best one was that the inmates had taken over the entire institution and were holding fifteen guards hostage and the governor was on his way. State troopers and the National Guard were lined up elbow-to-elbow on the walls and were preparing to lob tear gas into all the cell houses and shoot every single prisoner the minute the governor gave the word. There was no way this could be confirmed from where we were in K since the only view was of the other side of the institution across the quad, the chow hall, hospital, library, the top of the roof of the auto and metal shops, and a few other small buildings and offices. You couldn't see the walls or the towers from where we were; they were all behind our building where there weren't any windows.

"You're an idiot," I said to the guy who came up with this theory, a weight-lifter everybody called Clark Gable on account of the way his ears stuck out. I said it smiling. He was a mountain of muscles. "If they've taken over the joint how come we're still stuck in here? All I see out there are thirty guys running around like squirrels." It was true. For all the havoc they were creating over at the chow hall it looked like a small band of guys were doing all the destruction. Especially considering they had over two thousand of us locked up in here. It didn't look like any major riot, not like some I'd been in when every asshole in the place was out loose and running around.

Just when it looked like our friendly argument was going to develop into something unhealthy for yours truly, we heard a lot of yelling downstairs and then people running up the stairs. We all ran to the front. Across the way, the blacks were doing the same. In just seconds, there were fifteen-twenty guys outside our doors and they had hacksaws. The place went nuts.

Dusty grabbed me and Manny and pulled us aside.

"They get those doors open, the best thing to do is stay put. This riot is like every other fucking riot. Sooner or later the hacks will take the place back over and everyone who's out of their cell or dorm is either going to get shot or clubbed in the face or gassed and the ones that don't are going to the hole. Stay here and let these buttholes have their fun."

"He's right," I said to Manny. "The Man doesn't like it when this kind of shit happens. You don't want to be on the list when it's all over. Just stay up here when everybody goes out. We'll play some cards."

Good idea, except it didn't work out that way. Almost the very instant the bars on the doors were sawed through somebody started setting fire to the mattresses in the back of the dorm.

"Oh shit," we all said at the same time. Now we had to leave whether we wanted to or not, or else end up as Crispy Critters or die of smoke inhalation. We saw one of the arsonists come running up to the front, hollering and waving a rolled-up newspaper that was on fire, touching it to every pillow and blanket he ran by. It was ol' Clark Gable, the simple fuck, and I think I remember seeing his sheet when I worked in I.D. Arson. Just plying his trade. Smoke was rolling up behind him. He must have done a good job. We could already see the flames and our eyes were watering, not to mention we were hacking out pieces of lung with every breath. The door went down and guys were trampling each other trying to get out.

"Wait!"

Both Manny and I had started toward the gang that was killing themselves getting out of the dorm. We looked back at Dusty.

"Where you going?"

I looked at Manny, then back at Dusty and said, "Why, just out to stroll around the grounds. We figured that was better than getting toasted like a marshmallow."

"You guys got shanks?"

That *was* dumb. When I realized what I was about to do I hit the side of my head with an open palm. "Yeah, you're right, Dusty. Damn!"

Quickly, I ran down what we were talking about to Manny. "It ain't the hacks we got to worry about right now. It's other inmates. Half these bozos turn into sharks, this kind of shit goes down. Sharks that smell blood and go whacko. Some of these guys will cut you just because you're standing next to them or you look like their ex-wife." I looked closely at him, squinting my eyes. "Especially you, Manny. You for sure look like somebody's ex. I was you, I'd carry a bazooka."

Dusty ran over to his bunk and grabbed his pillow and began to rip the stitching. "Here!" He ran back over and pushed something in our hands. Laundry pins. One for each of us. Laundry pins are big brass pins they use to fasten the large canvas sacks they use for laundry. They look like Baby Huey's diaper pin and when you bend them out they make about a-foot-and-a-half-long shank. It's the favorite weapon for most of us, next to a filed-down spoon. They only let you have one eating utensil, a soup spoon, that you keep with you all the time. No knives or forks. You carry your spoon with you everywhere, twenty-four hours a day. Lots of guys hone down the handle on the concrete cell floors, sharpen it, and it makes a great weapon. Of course, you get caught with it, it's a week in the hole, so you try and cop an extra one, one that's for show and tell, just your regular spoon, and one you've made into a shank that you keep hidden.

There were lots of weapons in K Dorm. More than in the other cell houses because to get into K in the first place you had to have a squeaky-clean record. That meant they considered us less dangerous and less likely to be armed, so we didn't catch near as many shakedowns as the rest of the population.

I had such a spoon, taped inside one of the hollow legs of my bunk. I ran and got it, as well. You couldn't have too many weapons during a riot. Then we booked. Everybody else had already cleared out, and coming down the stairs we saw they'd set fire to the cell house below us, as well. There was no way the building would burn itself—it was solid concrete—but the danger was smoke inhalation.

We went outside, moved toward the middle of the compound between K and the chow hall. Guys were running everywhere, screaming and laughing and yelling and just going apeshit in general.

"Stick together, guys," Dusty said, and Manny and I shook our heads in agreement.

"Let's find out what's going down," Manny said, and Dusty reached out and grabbed the arm of a guy we knew, Baker, and yelled, "What's the situation, man?"

He ran it down for us.

It seems it all started over at the infirmary. "Big Alice," one of the weight-lifting drag queens, was there to get her finger looked at—she'd got it caught in a drill press over at the metal shop. When she asked for something for the pain the cheezy little Third World doctor just laughed and so Big Alice grabbed him and broke his arm. Then all hell broke loose, according to Baker.

It might have all ended there if the hack on duty had been around, but it turns out he was awol, having slipped over to the officer's mess to grab a quick sandwich. Guards aren't sup-posed to do that, leave their duty station, but they all did. When he came back, Alice and some of the other inmate patients grabbed him and threw him in a closet with the doc. They took his sandwich, too, Baker said. We all laughed at that.

From there it just escalated, he said. Two other hacks were walking by on their way to the front gate when one of them must have noticed something wrong at the hospital and decided to investigate. His buddy went on up to the gate and it was him that sounded the alarm, probably when he couldn't raise his partner on the walkie-talkie. His partner couldn't have called in as he was dead. By the time he walked into the hospital Big Alice and the rest of the cons there had broken into one of the drug cabinets and were all high as loons. They decided to get the guard high, too, and shot him full of Demerol—only they gave him a little bit more than what would be a safe dosage. He died happy, Baker said, and we all got another grin out of that.

From what we could figure from what Baker told us, it most likely could have ended right there but our lamebrain Warden, Mr. Coffey, pushed the panic button and hit the whistle, ordered all the inmates locked down, and the officers to come back up front until they could figure out exactly what was going on. That was a guess on our part, but it fit with what Baker told us. Coffey was a weasel from the git-go, always pulled bone-headed stunts like that. He blew their only chance to contain things before it became a riot. All he would of had to do was send about six of the biggest hacks with tear gas and the whole thing would have been history. Instead, he wasted enough time trying to make a decision that Alice and the hospital inmates recruited some others out in the yard, and it blew sky-high when the barber school guard, Jonesy, and Sniffles got shanked going into J. The inmates there grabbed Jonesy's keys and let out the whole damned block, and then the shit was in the fire. There was about fifty inmates locked up that all of a sudden weren't, and they ran over to the chow hall and started grabbing officers' steaks out of the reefer and cooking them. Naturally, it wasn't long before they started burning down the place, which we'd seen from our window at K earlier.

We looked around, dozens of guys running here and there, bunch of fucking baboons, and Dusty said, "Don't much look like the movies does it?" He said it to Manny.

No shit. In the movies, they have a riot, they make the convicts look like the Teamsters Union. Organized like nobody's business. Movie riots in the joint always have committees with lists of demands and all this strategy. Real riots aren't anything like that. Everybody's just shittin' and gittin', trying to grab all the goodies they can from each other, from the commissary, the chow hall, wherever, and guys go nuts trying to shank each other. Only people usually hurt are inmates. Usually by other inmates. I bet the doc and the guard over at the hospital were completely forgotten by Alice and the others, who were probably over at the commissary breaking down the wire cage to get at the cookie stash. Only reason the guards hadn't moved in yet was we had us a warden believed all that movie crap, was no doubt waiting for the Convict Committee to show up with their Twenty Demands. Like we didn't have but one demand. Let us the fuck out! Not much chance of that happening.

What they'd do is let us burn everything down, kill each other, and then early the next morning come in with the guns and dogs and shoot a few more of us. Most of us wouldn't be in any shape to resist. Twenty guys, for instance, would be working on making some quick apple jack to get drunk on while they had the chance. In fact, that sounded like a good idea to us.

"Fire's probably burned down in K by now," Dusty said. "Let's get our ass over to the chow hall and pick up some peaches and stuff and get loaded."

We booked over to what was left of the chow hall and sure enough there was a whole gang of guys loading up on fruit. We each loaded up a big bagful and headed back over to K.

The way you made apple jack was to scrub down the commode until it was squeaky clean, then you dumped a bunch of fruit and sugar and yeast in the water and let it set, three-four days, until it started to ferment. You skimmed off the fruit that was pretty ripe by then and drank what was left. Some good shit, made you insane it was so good. Only place you could brew apple jack was if you were in a cell. In the dorms, no way. There was only two toilets for about fifty guys and there was always a few pitched a bitch if you was to even hint you were gonna be using their crapper for that long. Besides, in a dorm was a boatfull of snitches would rat you out long before it was done and you'd end up in the hole and back in a cell house after they let you out.

We didn't figure we had three or four days to let the stuff brew naturally like it was supposed to, so Dusty said let's go over to the hospital and get some rubbing alcohol to speed things up.

There was a mob over there, must have had the same idea as we did. "Let's split up," Dusty said, when we saw two dozen guys with the same idea. "Everybody take a room and look for anything has alcohol in it. Grab as much as you can carry, and we'll meet back at the front door."

It was a good plan and we took off, each in a different direction. I went straight for the back of the building, seeing as how most guys were looking in the front offices. I figured if there was any alcohol up there they'd have found it by now, and if there was any left in the building it would be toward the back.

The first room I went into wasn't nothing but some kind of linen storage room. It only took five seconds to see they didn't keep anything but sheets and pillowcases and stuff like that in there, so I ran out and down the hall to the very last room. Nobody'd been there, as the door was still locked. A good sign. If the room was locked it meant there was something worth stealing there.

The door went down easy. I only had to hit it twice, and the whole door jamb splintered and I was in. I'd hit the mother lode. Up against the far wall was a long glass cabinet and I could see it was loaded with drugs and medication. Where the drugs were, the alcohol would be, too, and I was gonna load up with pills and stuff. If I could hide 'em good enough, I'd be rich when this all blew over. Plus, I had it in mind to get a little high myself.

I didn't mess around with the locks on the cabinets, just picked up a bedpan that was sitting on a counter and started bashing in glass. I went up and down the entire row of cabinets and busted out all the glass. I was looking around for a bag or something to put the bottles in when I heard something over by the door. I whirled around, sure it was one of the hacks—I was busted! I wish it had of been a guard. It was Frick, my old pal from the city lockup in Fort Wayne.

"Hey, chump," he said. "I been lookin' for you."

He had a shank in his hand, looked like a regular knife, not a homemade job like most. I wondered how he'd come to have a weapon like that.

FIFTEEN

We stood there a moment just staring at each other and all kinds of things went through my mind. Fear wasn't one of them. Oh, a bit I guess, but not much. My first thought was that he most likely wasn't aware I had a shank. Easy pickings is what he must see, standing there looking at me the way he was. Carve me up some honky I bet is what he was thinking. Otherwise, he would have just snuck up behind me, which would have been easy, all the noise I was making, breaking open cabinets. No, he figured I was unarmed so he'd have himself some fun, scare the honky, maybe fuck him.

I thought about taking him right then and there, and then I had another thought. At least ten guys saw me go back this way, not counting Manny and Dusty. There's gotta be one snitch in any ten guys, and if I fucked up this cocksucker back here, my ass would be in slam, guaranteed, and one more sentence to serve. No, I had to get him someplace else.

There was a back door just to my left, maybe three feet away. Out of the corner of my eye I could see the chain lock was off, but I didn't know if the regular door lock was on or off. I decided to chance it was unlocked. If it was locked, he'd be on me before I could unlock it and open it, but if I was in luck, I'd be out of there and he'd have to come after me. If worse came to worse, I'd take him on in the room and there was no doubt in my mind how that'd turn out. Dead nigger is how that would end.

Cool. It was unlocked. I was out the door before he knew what happened and booking across the yard toward the chow hall. I knew where I wanted to go and only hoped I could outrun him. My goal was the roof of the laundry.

I was halfway up the fire escape before I saw him and up over the top just as he was grabbing the bottom rung.

I don't think the little punk even knew what hit him. I think he was expecting to come up, chase me around a little bit, repeat our little tete-a-tete back at the city lockup, and then take me out, cut through the fine veins and capillaries of my neck. It didn't work out that way and I'm sure he was disappointed.

What happened was, when his head came up over the top I grabbed his fro and pulled him bodily the rest of the way up, at the same time I'm jabbing him with my straightened out laundry pin. He must have been one cocky sonofabitch 'cause he didn't even have his shank out yet, had it stuck in his back pocket. He fucked up. Like the old joke goes, "Don't bring one knife to a two-shank fight—especially if you're climbing up a fire escape and don't know what's waiting."

I must have went a little nutsy because I didn't nail him just once or twice, which would have done the trick. Instead, I performed needlepoint on him, punched a whole bunch of holes in his punk ass. I guess it was the music of his screams. Every time I stuck him he'd give out with an E-flat screech, and I played an inspirational kind of tune on my instrument. It felt so fucking good. I think I tried to poke him about as many times as he had me, back in city lockup. Maybe a few more. The only reason I finally quit was, in all honesty, my arm just got tired. I simply couldn't lift it one more time. Besides, he had shut up, wasn't playing the game anymore.

I looked around but I knew no one had seen us. Nobody else was on the roof, which was why I had headed there and

I was certain no one had seen us come up. Everybody was too busy robbing and pillaging each other.

First thing I did after I climbed down was walk over to the barber school. The inmates owned the institution, at least for a little while longer, and I could go just about anywhere I wanted. I had to get rid of my clothes, being as they were pretty nasty, what with the blood and all, and I kept an extra change at the school.

Once there, it was a piece of cake to bust a window in the door, reach in and unlock it. Inside, I shucked my bloody clothes, threw them on the floor of the shower stall and turned the cold water on. I remembered hearing someplace that cold water washes out blood better than hot. When they quit running red, I squeezed out the excess water and threw them out on the floor, adjusted the water so it was comfortable and stepped in, lathering down with shampoo all over. All the time I was doing this, I could hear guys running by outside, yelling and stuff. Drying off, I grabbed my extra jeans and shirt and dressed, grabbed the lump of wet clothes and took off. At the dumpster out back, I threw the wet clothes in and went off to find Dusty and Manny. As I passed by the chow hall, I took the laundry pin and dropped it on the grass in plain sight. Someone would find it and grab it I figured. Then, if there was an investigation and it turned up, it would turn up in someone else's possession, and heaven help him try and explain how he came to have it and where he was during the riot when Frick had bought it.

Pretty slick, I thought. Just your genius criminal mind at work.

I went back to the hospital, back to the room where I'd found the drugs. It was cleaned out. I hurried up to the front, looking in each room to see if Manny and Dusty were still there. They weren't. I didn't have a clue where they had gone so I just went out in the yard where there must have been five hundred inmates running around. Back and forth I went, but they weren't out in the yard, unless I missed them somehow. On a hunch I walked over to K Dorm and went inside and up to the dorm. The fires had died down and all there was was a little smoke in layers coming from some of the bunks in the rear. Dusty and Manny were sitting on his bunk with all kinds of shit spread out between them.

"Hey, where you been!" They looked up and grinned and pointed down to the stuff on the bed.

There must have been six dozen bottles of different pills and stuff piled up there. They were putting them in baggies and twisting them shut.

"Separate the uppers from the downers and put six in a bag," Dusty said. I jumped in and began sorting out bottles. When we were done, he told Manny to go stand by the door and keep watch.

"Anybody comes up, you let me know right now," he said. We gathered up an armful of baggies each and went over to the far wall. Dusty still had the same hiding place he'd had when I was in before, a concrete block that he pulled out from the back wall. It was a tight fit, but we got them all crammed into the space behind it. Before he replaced the block, he took the little can of gray paint he kept in the space and poured some on a paper towel. Putting the block back into place, he took his finger and repainted the lines around the block, filling in the gap. When he was done you couldn't tell the block had ever been out.

We went back over and sat down on his bunk, and Dusty reached up and pulled down a bag of the peaches we'd copped at the chow hall.

"You gonna make some apple jack?" I said.

"Naw. Let's just eat these. I got something better." He reached back in the bag and brought out a loaf of bread. I didn't understand what was so exciting about that until he reached back in the bag and pulled out a couple of bottles of aftershave. Aqua-Velva.

"Oh, man! This is great!"

"We're gonna get so-ooo drunk!" I said.

"On that?" Manny said.

"Yeah. Just watch."

Dusty and I grabbed our coffee cups and told Manny to get his, too. Dusty opened the bread and handed us each a stack. I held three pieces of bread over my cup, and Dusty began to pour the Aqua-Velva over it slowly.

"Hold it!" The stuff had started to eat a hole through the bread. I grabbed another stack and he began pouring again. It took six more slices before he emptied the bottle.

"What's that do?" Manny asked.

"Cuts the oil," Dusty said.

It wasn't Jack Daniels, but it did the job. After the first couple of sips it didn't even taste too bad. We finished both bottles.

"Now," he said. "Let's go turn ourselves in. I don't want to end up in the hole with the rest of these clowns, do you?"

We walked up to the front gate at the visitors' room, our fingers laced behind our heads, and sure enough, all the hacks were gathered there, milling around on the other side of the bars like a herd of cattle.

They acted tough, grabbing us and shaking us down, and even doing the body cavity routine, but we expected that. You could tell they were scared. I couldn't tell if they could see that we were half-drunk or not, not that I cared.

"How come your hands are sweaty?" I asked the hack who was having trouble getting his hand into a rubber glove. "This your first date?"

They put us in the officers' barber shop, along with about a dozen other inmates who had had the same idea, mostly old hands who knew what was coming. There was a window where you could see the parking lot outside the main administrative building. I knew then that time would slow down for a while when this was all over, with the memory of that view of freedom just inches away.

Most guys who've done any time at all will tell you that being in the joint is a thousand times easier than doing time in a city or county lockup. The reason is, in the joint you never see the outside. That may sound tough but believe me, it's far worse in most city jails where you can see the streets outside. All it does is remind you of where you're not. Outside, where you can go buy a beer, talk to a lady—shit— even turn on the TV and watch some stupid show. Freedom. The last thing you want when you've got a stretch of time to pull ahead of you is to be reminded of what you're missing. Inside the walls, you never see it, and you get so you can keep it from entering your mind, and time goes easy.

That's why guys hate to have to go testify at trials, which happens from time to time, when somebody gets killed inside. It means you have to climb in a van and get driven to some court, usually in Indianapolis, where you give your testimony. What's hard about it is you're on the road with regular folks, people on their way to their jobs or maybe to get laid, whatever. You see a car go by and there's a guy driving and a girl sitting next to him and then you see her bob down and you know what she's doing and it just kills you. For months afterward, that's all you think about. Some guys, though, they're just the opposite. Every chance they get to get out, trial, whatever, they're first on the bus. I guess they just like to torture themselves.

I remember the time right before I did my first bit, sitting in the South Bend city lockup staring out a window at the cars going by. Sundays were the worst because there wasn't much traffic or people going by, and when they did, like, say a couple walked by arm in arm beneath you, you had plenty of time to fantasize about where they were going, what they were going to be doing, and here you sat with your willie in your hand, and it sure wasn't going to be the same and wouldn't be for a long, long time.

Jail time just murders you. Give me six months in the joint where I don't have to be reminded of what's out there to one day in jail where all you see is assholes walking around, taking for granted what you'd give your left nut for. I'll take six months in a real joint over six days in the classiest city lockup there is.

I tried to stay away from that window in the officers' shop, but couldn't help myself. It just kept pulling me over. Every five minutes I'd get up off where I was sitting on the floor and wander over and look out.

After a while, Dusty said, "You're fucking up, you know, dontcha?"

I knew, I knew. Still, it was like some kind of forbidden fruit you know is bad for you but which you can't help eating. Must be how a junkie feels, why they keep sticking that needle in their arm even though they aren't stupid—they know they're killing themselves, but man! how sweet the poison!

We spent the night on the floor, about fifteen of us, and the officers brought in pillows and blankets. They even brought us in Big Macs from the town's MacDonald's. They were cold time we got them, but who cares? They were delicious. Freedom food.

Along about daybreak it got quiet. All night we could hear the murmur of officers outside the barber shop and then it got deadly still just before the sun came up. That meant one thing. They'd gone in to take back over the institution.

"We'll be back in our bunks before noon," Dusty predicted.

Actually, it was almost three in the afternoon before they

came and took us back down to K. It seems they found a guy up on the roof of the laundry with a bunch of holes in him and once they got everybody rounded up and locked down they brought in the state police crime lab boys to check it out. They kept us up front until the state boys were done.

Going back inside, we passed a group of guards and I overheard one of the hacks say to another, "Can you believe this shit? Guy's got thirty-three stab wounds and he's still alive!"

Fuck me.

SIXTEEN

We were talking about two days later, Manny and me, while we were playing double sol, about the joint and shit that went down, and we were discussing prison movies and books and crap like that.

Movies about prison just gripe my ass. They've got about five standard types they always show that I've never met. It's like movies about the service. I was in the Navy before I got sent up and I've never seen guys there that look the least like the ones they've got up there storming Iwo Jima or wherever. Those guys in the flicks are all drop-dead hunks in their late twenties. Well, color me orange, but when I was sailing the ocean blue, all my mates seemed to be skinny, and we all looked like we were sixteen, and it was hard to make out our features through all our pimples. I guess Hollywood doesn't think kids look like soldiers. In movies, anyway—in real life that's what you get—punk-ass kids who get drunk on three beers and throw up on you and want to fight every five minutes, only they ain't much good at it.

It's like when Manny and I were up in Quarantine before we got released into the population. We're hanging out on the walk one day just before they locked us down after supper, and I spot this clown who came in the day I did.

"Punk," I thought, and I must have said it out loud 'cause Manny says, "Huh?"

"That guy," I said, pointing him out. He was in a cell

aways down from mine, standing around jiving with some black dude.

"Whaddya mean? You know him?"

"Naw," I said. "I just know his type. White bread motherfucker. His daddy sells insurance and his mommy's president of the PTA. He's about to get his asshole reamed. Saturday morning when we go to the movie he's gonna be roaming the aisles for his daddy, giving B.J.'s for packs of tailormades. I can read him like a D.C. comic upside down."

"Yeah," said Manny after a minute. "He ain't right, is he?"

Even Manny could make the guy, and it's Manny's first time doing hard time. Reason Manny could was he was an outlaw, same as most of the rest of us, even if he hadn't done joint time before.

Just the way this guy stood, the way he acted, you could tell he was a goner. The sissies would swoop on him like they was pigeons and he was a bread crust just hit the sidewalk.

"I had a guy like him was my first cellmate first time here," I told Manny. "This guy could be his twin."

This guy, name of Rudy or some such silly handle, had done crimes, sure, else he wouldn'ta been there, but he wasn't like any of the rest of us. I had him scoped out in ten minutes and it turned out later I was right. About three days later it came down. It's hard to bullshit a bullshitter, to sell wolf tickets to Sonny Liston, as we say. This kid was basically a lonely kid, born not to bucks maybe but to your standard-issue middle class family, and it was as if he looked around one day and figured out what was "cool" to him and then tried to fake it, to fit in with a group he thought was hip. And, even though he "walked the walk" and "talked the talk" it was all a front. See, he was an actor and could take his observations and use them, play a role, but you knew it wasn't real *inside*—he just plain didn't feel it deep down, and naturally, the way the rest of us did. He had a bad end coming, I could of made money betting on it—a black mother "befriended" him—I warned him, but you could see he had it in his mind he'd really hit the mother lode by being "accepted" by one of the baddest badasses, as if that would rub off on his puny ass and make him the same—only he ended up being the guy's kid in about as long a time as it takes to get the lid off the KY jelly tube. After that, the guy turned him out, used to take him out nights in the TV room and send him around jacking guys off and giving out blow jobs for Camels, and then when he got tired of his shit, threw him off the third tier and squashed his monkey ass like a rotten coconut. The reason he got tired of him was the kid "fell in love" and every other minute was crying he loved this guy and turn around five minutes later and say he was going to kill himself. The black guy got tired of his soap opera—it gave him a headache—and so he erased him.

This guy in quarantine reminded me of that other guy exactly. Where's this guy in your prison movies? Oh, yeah—sometimes they get somebody like Sal Mineo to play somebody kind of like that but then there's always somebody else like Tony Curtis bails his weak ass out. Yeah, sure. Like anybody else gives a shit. Like somebody in the joint looked like Tony Curtis could bail *anybody's* ass out. Guy looked like that would be the cleanest guy in the joint on account of all the group showers he was gonna have to be taking.

Or—better yet—they have Sidney Poitier saving this clown. First time I see a black guy sticking up for a white guy in here they better put both of 'em in the hold for safekeeping.

I didn't know what I was going to do about Frick. His real name was Freddy Boles, I found out, from the prison newspaper that had an article on it.

They got him over in Indianapolis, at Methodist Hospital, got him handcuffed to a bed in the security ward and so far he hasn't come to, it says in the paper. I've got two chances to skate here. One, he doesn't make it, croaks before he comes to, and two, if he doesn't become room temperature, he doesn't snitch me out.

You'd think I'd want him dead just on general principles but that wasn't the case. My mad was gone, completely erased. That was weird. Guy does what he done to me, you'd think I'd want him in a box and sure; that's what I wanted originally, only now I didn't really care. The only thing I didn't want was to end up doing more time.

I'm still trying to work out what I was going to do about Boles if and when he came back to Pendleton, when we got some good/bad news.

Bud was on his way back!

SEVENTEEN

"Mayes! You got a visitor."

It was the hack Franklin. I was lying on my bunk trying to read Moby Dick on Sunday afternoon and had just got past all the whale shit and about to get to the good stuff when Franklin called out my name. I'd read this book three-four times already; it was one of the few decent things they had in the library. Mostly what they had was westerns and kids' books. Hardly any covers on any of them. Guys would rip off the covers so they had something to look at in their cells.

It was my brother.

"Hey, Ray," I said and shook his hand. This was a surprise. I think it was only the second or third time any of my family had ever come down to see me. Not that I could blame them. It was about a three- or four-hour drive from South Bend.

"I put some money on your account," he said. "Fifty bucks. I figured you could use it." That was a double surprise. The last time Raymond gave me anything, pigs still had the ability to fly.

"I sold one of your coats for a hundred," he said. "I figured half was yours."

I thanked him and we just sat there looking at each other for a minute or two.

Normally, I hated getting visitors. All a visit from someone on the outside did was remind you where you were and where you weren't. It fucked you up when they left, knowing they were going to get in a car and drive away, free as the wind, and you were going to go back and sit in your fucking cell and give names to your toes. The worst kind of visit is the one from your lady. All you can think of is that when she leaves she's gonna be hitting the sheets with some mother-fucker. That kind of shit can really fuck you up.

This visit didn't feel like that, though. In fact, it felt pretty good. Ray was all right, a pretty good dude, matter-of-fact. He'd even gone on a job or two with us, a penny-ante burglary or two, but then he got scared of what could happen and quit. That was all right. Some are just not cut out for the outlaw life and Ray was one of them. Not enough of the right kind of guts. Oh, regular things, like fighting, there was no one had more balls than Ray—I seen him take on two guys at once lots of times and there's no one else I'd rather have beside me in a bar brawl—but breaking into a bar at three in the morning? That took a different kind of cojones, the kind Raymond didn't have.

Our visitors' area wasn't like anything you see in the movies, with glass partitions and headphones where you talked to your visitor. It was just a large room, up toward the front of the institution, and it was laid out with two rows of chairs facing each other. At the back of the room there was a high podium and a hack stood back there, looking down on all of us while another guard walked around to make sure you weren't doing anything funny. You could touch your visitor, hug and kiss them, stuff like that. I looked down the row and saw guys trying to do more with their girlfriends and wives. Cop a feel, stuff like that. The hack walking around would let them get away with some stuff, to a point. You could feel your girl's boob, if you were quick and not too obvious, but then again, that depended on who the hack was who was walking around. Some were decent about that kind of thing but others would crack on you right now.

"Mom's dead."

I hadn't been paying attention and I had to ask Ray what he said again.

"Mom. She died. Day before yesterday."

I couldn't get what he was saying.

"I was going to write you and then thought that would be a lousy way to break the news to you so I came on down."

I didn't say anything, just sat there staring at Ray.

"I asked the warden for you, if you could get out to go to the funeral. He said he'd consider it. The funeral's day after tomorrow, on Tuesday."

"What'd she die of?" is what I finally said.

"It was her heart. Heart attack. The doctor said she probably didn't feel a thing since she was asleep when it happened."

Yeah, right. Your heart seizes up, you don't feel a thing. I'm gonna buy that shit. Fucking doctors, fucking *everybody*, always lying to you. Fucking punk doctor. Everybody was a punk.

We talked a little bit more, some stuff about when we were kids and things Mom had said or done and then Ray said he had to leave. Ruthy Ann was in the car, waiting.

"Why didn't she come in?" I already knew the answer to that. My sister-in-law hated my guts, thought I was a "bad influence" on Ray.

"She couldn't handle it. Too depressing, she said. She sent her love."

I'm sure, I thought, but I didn't say that to Ray.

"Well, that's what I came down for, mainly. Let you know and give you the money."

We stood up and hugged and the walking guard came over.

"Visiting hours aren't over," he said. "You still got a half hour."

"I got to get back to my cell," I said. "I'm expecting an important phone call from the Pope." We shook hands, Ray and I, and I turned and walked to the back door. In a minute, the guard on the other side came up and unlocked it and I went through. I looked back and saw Raymond's back going through the other door. He turned around and waved, and I waved back, and then the hack had me put my hands up on the wall while he shook me down.

Later that afternoon, Warden Coffey came down to K himself and had me brought downstairs to talk to me.

"I checked your packet," he said. "Pretty clean, Mayes. I think I can let you go to your mother's funeral."

"No thanks," I said.

EIGHTEEN

Dusty found out first, about Bud coming back. It was a week after the riot had ended. Things were pretty much back to normal, except we had a shakedown every time we turned around and you didn't want to be one of the guys in solitary. The hacks down there were having a ball, thumping on the prisoners sorry enough to find themselves there, especially the ones that were there because of the riot.

There was two hacks, brothers, worked the midnight shift in the hole, were total sadists. Big motherfuckers, they weren't twins or anything, although they both joined the staff on the same day about six years before. There was four years in age between them but they looked like twins. Big bastards, about six-three and about a pound apart at two-fifty. Most hacks, they try to stay away from the hole, but not the Delaney brothers. They loved it. Didn't mind a bit they had to listen to inmates screaming all night. In fact, if they weren't screaming they'd roust one out and play their favorite trick. One of them would hold the inmate down and the other one would pick up the end of one of those heavy wooden benches down there and drop it on the poor sucker's head. They'd done it so many times to one inmate in partic-ular, Betty Sue, that she was brain-scrambled. Betty Sue got to liking what the Delaney's did to her, fucked up all the time on purpose just to get back in the hole, get her head smacked again. It's a wonder they didn't kill her, all the bumps to the noggin they gave her, but she just smiled goofy all the time and kept coming back for more. I think she thought the Delaneys were her mom and dad, and them whacking on her brain meant they loved her. Her real name was Steve McQueen, like the actor—I knew that from my time in I.D.—but I doubt anybody else knew her real name.

Just thinking about the Delaneys was enough to keep me on the straight and narrow, like it was most of us.

But other than the shakedowns and more guys spending time in the hole, things were pretty normal. Oh yeah, the chow was lousier even than usual, being as how a lot of the food got stolen during the riot and they weren't about to replace it. For a while, we got powdered eggs three meals a day for a week or so and then they gave us a break and served beans three squares per day, but nobody gave much of a fuck about that. Regular chow wasn't much better. It wasn't like we got prime rib ever anyway.

Dusty came over to me at the barber school the third morning we're back to normal and I could tell he was excited.

"Bud's coming back!" he said.

At first, I didn't get what he was saying, who he was talking about.

"Bud who?" I said, like a dummy.

He gave me this look and then I knew who he was talking about.

"How'dja know?"

"Jonesy told me. He got a call from his sister, lives in Fort Wayne." Jonesy was the hack got us into the barber school first time and that got stabbed in the riot. Great guy, one of the few hacks everybody liked, guards and inmates alike. Square guy, didn't mess with your head like a lot of them try to. Black guy, too, but regular. It was a shame he'd got stabbed, but that's what goes down in shit like that. Most of us were glad he hadn't bought it.

Turned out the news was right on. Bud was being tried next week in Superior Court for killing his girlfriend. I guessed that would be Kimmie, although Jonesy didn't know any names. He came over to K Dorm that night and told us what he knew. Showed us the stitches where he'd been cut in his throat. He'd lost some blood, which saved his life on account of he'd passed out and the assholes who cut him thought he was dead, but mostly what they'd cut was neck muscle. Turns out Bud smacked Kimmie a little harder than he meant to and she cracked her head on the floor, according to what Jonesy had heard.

"Way it looks, they got him nailed for manslaughter," Jonesy said. "I expect you'll be seeing him in a couple two or three weeks maybe."

For some reason, this got me to thinking about Donna again. What with all that had gone down, the riot, Mom, and my problems with Boles, I had pretty much put her out of my mind, but thinking about Bud and Kimmie got me to remembering about the trip Bud and me took to Louisiana, and that got me to remembering about why I had gone there in the first place.

What I got to thinking about was screwy. It wasn't pictures of me and Donna in bed, shit like that, but what it was was about how different we were in a lot of ways.

Like memory. Donna had this fantastic memory. She could tell you what her teacher's name was in first grade. Me? I wouldn't bet a nickel on what state we were living in when I was in first grade, much less what my teacher's name was, or even what she looked like. It could of been a man for all I remember.

My whole past is like that. I don't know—is that normal? I mean, I remember *things*, not a lot of them, but a few. It's not always things that were important, either. Donna said I couldn't remember because my childhood was so horrible I had blocked it out, but that's bullshit. I just had so many things happen nobody could remember them all.

I told Donna there was nothing to block out. My folks didn't beat me that much, not more than anybody else's folks. Dad didn't believe in spanking you if you were a boy, anyway. When you messed up, he'd say, "Okay cowboy, you think you can take your old man, come on." He'd want you to fistfight him. My sister Janice, he'd take his belt to her. Not to me. Me, he wanted me to fight him. If I did, doubled up my fists and attacked him, he'd bust me in the chops, put me on my ass. If I didn't, he'd call me a sissy and laugh at me, tell my mom to get out a dress for his little girl. I don't know which was worse, getting clopped in the puss or getting called a girl.

It was that kind of shit made me move out of the house when I was sixteen, I told Donna.

"I slept in my car for two years and finished high school. Once in a while, somebody would let me stay with them, but mostly I just lived out of my car. I'd go into the high school early in the morning and wash up."

"How'd you get money to eat?"

I just smiled at her.

NINETEEN

"So that was a riot."

Me, Manny and Dusty were sitting on his bunk while Dusty did his books. He was king shit now on account of all the dope he had to sell. We were all getting rich. I had three hundred in green myself, not to mention all the cookies and cigarettes I wanted. Dusty treated you right. So far, I hadn't had to do much. Threaten a guy once in a while. One guy, we jacked up, Manny and I, broke some teeth out, shit like that. Scared him. He paid up. It was an easy job.

Manny was talking about the riot.

"Yeah, that's pretty much it," said Dusty, toting up figures in a long column. "That's what a riot's all about."

"What'd you think a riot was like?" I asked Manny.

"I don't know…something more, I guess."

"That was a pretty typical one," I said. "Guys go nuts, grab a hack if they can, burn everything in sight and shank their best friend. The warden lets it go on a few days for political reasons."

"Whaddya mean?"

I explained how it worked.

"The warden knows he can shut most any riot down in five seconds but he doesn't. He calls up the papers, the governor, people like that, tells 'em he's got a serious situation on his hands, gets interviewed by everybody and his brother. Newspapers, TV, you name it. Milks that puppy like a big ol'

Holstein. Then, he sends in about fifty hacks with shotguns and tear gas, and it's all over in about five minutes. He coulda done that at the gitgo but then he wouldn't get all that wonderful publicity. Now, he looks like some kind of hero to the straights. They think he's this tough mother-fucker on crime, criminals."

"You're shittin' me."

"Yeah? Didn't it go down just like I laid it out?"

It had, too. Soon as the Man moved in with the twelve gauges, guys laid down their shanks all over the place, fought each other to get in line and give themselves up. It was a riot ending the riot.

Just then there was a commotion up by the front door, and it opened and in came four guards.

"Manuel Del Rio, get your ass up here!"

They even put the cuffs on Manny before they took him away. That was serious when they did that.

The dorm went nuts after they left with Manny, every-body wondering what the fuck he'd done.

Dusty thought somebody'd snitched us out for the dope we were selling. I hoped he was right but I had a pretty good idea that wasn't it. Sure enough, back he came in about four hours, and he was about as white-faced as a Mexican could get. Right away he came for me and got me off back in a corner.

"That guy was stabbed?" he said. "They think *I* done it."

"What guy?" I said, playing dumb.

"Don't fuck with me, Jake." He was mad, really mad.

"Okay, okay, I know what guy. Why'd they think you did it?"

"Why? Oh, gee, I don't know. Maybe it's because I held him over the rail in Quarantine till he shit his pants."

"They don't know that was you," I said. They didn't, either. If they'd seen who did it that time, Manny would have got sent to the hole right away. I told him that.

"Yeah. You're right there, buddy. Somebody snitched me out but I played dumb. Kept telling them it wasn't me. They don't believe me but there ain't much they can do. It's my word against whoever snitched me out."

"That's good, Manny. Just hang tough. There ain't much they can do." He was a standup guy, for sure, and I didn't think I had to worry about him cracking, but I did feel bad he had to go through this on my account. I decided to level with him.

"It was me lit up that punk," I said. "But if you hang in there they'll never know. This'll all blow over." I told him when and how I did it and he remembered. I didn't tell him why.

"Yeah, that's right. Me and Dusty wondered where you'd got off to. I shoulda figured it was you done him. Only I didn't know his name. Well, this is some shit, bro, but don't worry—I'm not gonna snitch you out."

I thanked him and I meant it, and then I had a twinge of conscience. "Manny, there's something you ought to know." I wasn't sure if I should tell him this, but decided I owed it to him. "They can't prove anything, sure, but you don't tell them what you know, there's probably gonna be some trouble for you. You might not make parole first time out. Maybe they work you over sometime."

"Aw, shit, Jake. I can take whatever they dish out. I don't give a fuck if they beat me even. It won't be the first time the Man took a poke at me. I'm Mexican, remember? That's our job—get fucked with by the Man." His whole attitude changed; now he was my friend, proud of how he'd handled the interrogation, hadn't weakened.

"No, Manny, this may 'cause you serious trouble," I said. "No matter if they don't do anything, they can still fuck you up another way. This'll go in your jacket and when you come up for parole they'll use it against you. You'll probably get denied, first time. In fact, I'd bet on it."

It was the truth. They couldn't get at a guy one way, they always had his parole they could fuck with. And they usually did.

He got serious again. "How can they do that? They can't prove nothing."

I ran it down for him. "Manny, this is the joint. They don't have to prove anything."

He saw I was right. "You think I'll have to do my whole bit?" He was on a one-to-ten, should make parole in ten months, this hadn't happened.

"No, they'll probably deny you the first time, figure that's enough punishment." I wasn't blowing smoke, saying that. That was about the way the warden's mentality worked. "Keep your nose clean the rest of the way and you'll make it the next time up."

"Six more months, you're saying."

"Yeah."

He was quiet for a minute or two. Then, he said, "Fuck it. Piece of cake. I'm your man, Jake."

I could of hugged him, I loved that guy so much right then. He was willing to give up six months of his freedom for me and we hardly knew each other. Before Pendleton we'd been casual acquaintances, nothing more. He knew what it meant. He was giving up six months for the four or five or more years I'd end up doing if they found out who shanked Boles. More, if he died. What do you say to a guy like that?

"I won't forget this, Manny."

"I know," is all he said.

We talked some more about Boles and came to the conclusion that either he hadn't come to yet down there in the hospital in Indy, or else he was keeping his mouth shut. So far, anyhow. Who knows what he'd do once he got back here, provided, of course, that he lived. I knew what I was going to have to do if he came back. Ice him. I couldn't take a chance on him deciding one fine day he was going to snitch me out. Even if he didn't, he would own me. I'd rather do a hundred years in solitaire than have him or any other punk own me.

From then on Manny and I were like brothers. They didn't question him anymore and they never came for me or Dusty. We figured they thought they'd find out what happened when Boles came back to the joint, soon as he was well enough to be transported back. I'd have to find a way to get over to the infirmary, which is where they'd keep him till he healed all the way.

I told Manny about Donna. Not even Dusty or Bud knew what had happened, why I'd tried to kill myself that time.

"She stabbed this girl," I said. I don't know why I was telling him all this, stuff I hadn't even told Bud. "This other girl I dated a couple of times. We'd broke up for about the twentieth time, me and Donna."

TWENTY

I told Manny the whole story. We were staying in, on a Saturday morning while everyone else went to the movie. Sat up at the front table, playing double sol and eating Keebler's Chocolate Chips and smoking Camels.

"I was hung up on her, bro," I said, trying to explain it to him. "She owned my ass."

"I been there," he said, and the way he said it I knew it was true.

"We got in this fight one time. Hell, we were always getting in fights." I laughed, remembering. "I was back in the bedroom and she pulled out her gun from her purse and fired it at me. It's a good thing she's a lousy shot 'cause she missed me about twenty feet. Put a hole in the living-room ceiling. How bad a shot is that? Anyway, I made a run for her, tackled her like she was a ball carrier, and got the gun away from her. Gave her a swat. Maybe a couple. Then, the cops came. Somebody, probably downstairs, called 'em. They took me away. I coulda told them she shot at me but it was an unregistered gun and I didn't want to get her in trouble. I figured they'd keep me overnight and let me go, which is what they did. But that was it. I figured it was all over. How can you live with a bitch shoots at you? I'd never trust myself to fall asleep!" We both got a hoot out of that.

"Soon as I got out of jail I came over and got my stuff and booked, mate. Got me an apartment over off Lake. You know those ones by all those doctors' offices?

"I started taking out some other ladies," I went on. "One weekend, a Sunday, I must have had four different chicks come over, different times, got laid each time. I was having a ball but it was crazy. No matter how much fun I was having, I still couldn't get Donna out of my mind. I was fucked up, man.

"Anyway, the last chick left about eleven that night and I went to bed. To sleep." Manny cracked up, leaned back in his chair and laughed with his mouth wide open.

"I guess you weren't gonna pound your trouser worm," he said.

"I guess not. I was just getting asleep when the doorbell rang and I got up and it was Donna. 'I got to talk to you,' she said.

"Fuck, Donna, I said. I'm just about asleep. We're over, sugar. Why don't you just leave me alone. 'No,' she said, 'I've really got to talk to you.'

"Well, I said, I'm just about asleep and if I don't go right back to bed I won't be able to. I oversleep and lose this job my P.O.'ll violate me.

"'Okay,' she said, pushing her way in. 'You go back to bed. I'll come with you and we'll talk in the morning. It's really important.'"

I looked over at Manny. "You know how it is when you're just about asleep? I told her, all right, come on in but we're not doing anything, Donna. I just want to go to sleep.

"Well, she came in and I went back and climbed in bed and she came in a minute later and crawled in with me, buck naked. I meant what I said, though, I wasn't going to fuck her. I turned over and closed my eyes, tried to get to sleep again. About five minutes later the doorbell rang again.

"It was a girl I'd seen a couple of times that week. Patsy. 'Patsy,' I said, 'I've got company.' 'Oh,' she said, 'That's cool. I'll see you tomorrow then.' And she left.

"When I came back into the bedroom, Donna jumped up and asked me who that was. Nobody, I said, just a friend. She's gone. Donna ran to the front door and must have seen her walking away. She came back and she was hot.

"'You're fucking that girl,' she said. I said, No, I'm not but that's none of your business anyway. We're broke up, I said.

"'That's it,' she said, slamming around and throwing her clothes on. 'I'm outta here.' That was the original idea, I said, back to her, and she went out, just about busting the door.

That's it, I'm thinking, and went back and laid down. But then I thought I heard voices and got up and opened the door, and sure enough, there's Patsy sitting in a chair by the pool and Donna's giving her holy hell.

"'Donna!' I yelled down. 'Get your ass out of here right now or I'm calling the cops.' I didn't say anything to Patsy, even though I knew she didn't have a clue what was going on, but I knew Patsy was cool. I figured if I said anything to her that'd fire Donna up again and I'd just tell Patsy the next day what went down and she'd understand. Well, they both get up and head for their cars. Patsy always parked on one side of the complex. I watched for a minute, saw Donna was heading in a different direction and went back inside. I lay back down but then I got to thinking—I know this bitch—Donna—I better be sure she's left.

"I went to the front door again, and sure enough, Donna's dogging Patsy, walking right behind her, yapping at her. I ran out of the apartment along the catwalk. All I had on were my jockeys. There's a little space where you can look out at the parking lot and I ran to that. Patsy's up against a car and Donna's giving her the business. I ran downstairs and around the corner, and just as I came around the corner,

I see Donna's hand go up and she smacked Patsy. She smacked her hard, dude. I never seen a *guy* hit another guy the way that broad hit her. I ran over to them and just as I got there Donna's raising her hand to smack Patsy again. Only she wasn't hitting her. She was stabbing her. It really didn't register, though. I got there just as she was coming down with the knife and I grabbed her arm with one hand and Patsy with the other and shoved them apart. Donna went down on her knees and then started coming up, trying to cut me. I ducked my stomach back and at the same time grabbed her hand with the knife and hit it against my knee. This all happened fast, man. Really fast.

"She lost the knife when her hand hit my knee and my first thought is to find the knife. I know if I get the knife first she can't hurt me. We're both scrabbling around looking for it—it was dark in that parking lot—and I find it first. It was this big-ass switchblade—in fact, I'd given it to her a long time ago as a present—and I find it and pick it up and she sees I've got it and she took off running. I'm standing there with this knife and I tried to close it and couldn't, as it's bent in two places. I just stand there until I see the reflection of her lights go on in the other parking lot and hear her tires burn out, and then I walk over to Patsy, who's standing up against a car.

"Well, this sounds weird, but it's the truth, Manny. I've got this knife in my hand and everything but it still doesn't dawn on me that Patsy's been stabbed. It just happened so fast. She didn't know she'd been cut, either.

"I walk up to her and say, 'Are you all right?' She's got this white silk blouse on and chinos and I see little tiny sprinkles of blood on the blouse, looked like somebody'd sprinkled red salt out of a shaker, or Tabasco sauce...yeah...more like Tabasco sauce. 'You been hit,' I said. 'You got a nosebleed.' 'No,' she says, 'She missed me. I ducked and she hit me in the back.'

"She turned around, and man! Her whole back was solid red and blood was running down her pants like she was peeing herself. 'You been stabbed,' I said, what had happened finally dawning on me. 'I have?' she said. She didn't even know it herself."

Just then, the dorm hack came by, motioned at us to come over. He was taking the count. Even though he knew us, he made us tell him our names and he read the numbers off our shirts, made checkmarks on his clipboard and then left, probably to take a nap downstairs where his desk was.

We went back and sat down at the table.

"You sure you want to hear the rest of this?" I asked Manny.

"Fuck yes," he said, grinning. "This is some wild bitch!"

I went ahead with the story.

"Well, I wanted to take her over to Parkview Hospital, but she said no. She wanted us to go up to my apartment and get a better look at where she'd been stuck. We climbed up the stairs and I'm thinking she's not that bad, being as how she can go up stairs and all. When we get to my apartment I took off her blouse and all I can see is an entry wound about this big"—I held up my fingers to show a width of about an inch and a half or so—"so my mind says the knife only went in a couple inches and hit a bone. That's what bent the blade, I'm thinking. Anybody knows you can bleed a lot from even a small cut. The blood's not running any more, it's kind of just bubbling a little. I bandage her up with a bath towel and some electricians' tape I had, and then she says maybe I ought to take her over to the hospital, as she's feeling a little woozy. That's smart, I tell her, and we go downstairs. I want to take her in my car but she said she wanted me to drive her over in her car. If she leaves her car there she said, Donna might come back and fuck with it. That wasn't the reason, only I didn't know that at the time. What it was, Patsy ran drugs for this guy, mostly grass, and she had a couple garbage bags full in the trunk. What I found out later, she was afraid the cops might find it if they came to check out things.

"So, anyway, I drive her over to Parkview and pull up to the emergency room entrance and the rent-a-cop comes out and they get a wheelchair after I tell them the score and wheel her in. I don't see her until the next morning.

"I tell the rent-a-cop what's gone down and he calls the real deal, and when that guy gets there, a uniform, I tell him the same story and give him the knife. I tell him where he can probably find Donna. Look over at the North Star Bar on State, I say. How's the girl got stabbed, he asks, and I tell him I don't know, I don't think it's that bad, and give him my reasoning about hitting the bone and all. But check with the doctor, I said.

"Well, he doesn't check with the doctor, just leaves and they pick up Donna the next morning and all she gets charged with is simple assault, not assault with a deadly weapon or attempted murder or any of that, only I don't know none of this until the next day.

"About an hour after I bring Patsy in, I'm sitting by my lonesome in the waiting area and in comes this lady and man. The man looks exactly like that guy used to be on *Miami Vice*, the TV show? You know, the captain? The one with all the acne scars? Remember? Anyway, this lady comes over to me, no howdy-do, nothing, and she says, 'If my little girl dies, you die, and this guy will kill you.' She means the scar-face with her. It must be Patsy's mom I guess, which it is, and I try to explain how it isn't my fault—that if it wasn't for me, Patsy probably would be dead, as Donna was fixing to stab her again when I broke it up.

"'Don't matter none,' she says. 'If she hadn't been at your

place she wouldn't have got stabbed to begin with.' I guess she'd already talked to the cops or the hospital or somebody, got the lowdown on what happened. You couldn't reason with her. This guy she was with, later I find out he's connected, would of done what she said, terminated my ass. Him, I never talked to. In fact, the whole time, the four hours we sat there, the only ones in the waiting room, he never said a word to me or her. Just sat there mugging on me. It was creepy.

"I went to the john a couple of times and each time I'm thinking, Should I just take off now, go to California or something? See, I was convinced that if Patsy died her mom meant business. There was no doubt in my mind. The only thing kept me there was I still thought Patsy wasn't hurt all that much.

"Shit. It was serious all right. Along about daybreak this doctor comes out to talk to us. 'We think she's gonna make it,' he says to Patsy's mom, 'but it's still a little shaky.' Turns out the knife went all the way in, almost came through the other side. It did hit a bone and that's what saved her. 'We were looking to see if the blade hit the lung,' he said. 'If it had even nicked it, we couldn't have saved her. Her lungs would have filled up with blood and she would have basically drowned.' As it was, they had ended up giving her a six-pack of blood, and the doc said she died on them twice, and they had to bring her back from the dead. They had to wait until the blood clotted and moved away from the lung to get a clear picture. The x-ray showed it had missed, but how he didn't know. It was a miracle.

"For her *and* me. Once we found out she was out of the woods, we all left. Before we did, her mom turned to me and said, 'You're still on the hook, Mayes. She might still die. If she does, you're dead, mister.'

"Way it turned out, Patsy came through fine, although she was a little sore."

"So why'd you try to kill yourself? I don't get it."

"Wait a minute. I'm getting to it." I seen Manny was getting antsy now that the bloody part was all over so I speeded up a couple of the in-between details and cut to the grand finale. "Patsy gets out of the hospital, sore but okay, and we even started dating kinda heavy, although we had to fuck real easy or else open up her wound again. Her mom decides she likes me and she tells me what she told me in the hospital was for true—I'da been dead meat if her darlin' daughter'd croaked. She says she's glad she didn't 'cause now she likes me, but somehow that didn't make me feel a whole lot better. She's an okay enough gal, but every time I see her I still get a little nervous.

"Anyhoo, a couple weeks go by and then I start getting phone calls at work from Donna. She don't say hello, kiss my ass or nothing when I pick up the phone, just starts talking like we hadn't ever stopped. 'I drive by your work every day when I get off,' she says, 'and I point my gun at you while I'm going by. One of these days I'm pulling the trigger, motherfucker.' The first time or so she pulls this I just sort of laugh it off, but after a solid week of these kinds of conversations I had enough and called the prosecuting attorney. 'Nothing we can do,' he says, 'until she does something, but I made a note of this sir, and if she ever actually shoots at you or anything like that, we'll pick her up.' That made me feel about as good and safe as finding out I got blood in my urine. I thought once or twice that maybe I ought to do her before she does me, but when I start scheming about how to carry that off, I realize I'm still fucked up over her."

"You still fucked up over this crazy bitch after the shit she done?" I didn't realize Manny's eyes could get that wide. The way he looked and the way he said it made me think maybe it was me that was crazy. "How can you even want to be on the same planet with her?"

"Because I'm stupid?"

I wasn't a hundred percent joking. I stared at the end of the cigarette I had going.

"Yeah. It's somethin', huh? Go figure. You want me to lie about it?"

"Naw, man. It's just…well, I don't figure you to be pussy-whipped, that's all."

"You wait, Manny. Anyway, I didn't know what to do. I knew she was just about wacko enough to pull some stunt like that—drive by and shoot me—it wouldn't be hard—I'm working in front of this big plate glass window two feet from the street—and then I get this phone call from her."

"What'd she say?" He was all ears.

"She said, 'I just want to tell you why I came over that night.'

"That's right. You said she said she wanted to talk to you about something."

"Yeah. What it was, what she said was that she was pregnant and that she murdered it. That's the words she used."

"You mean—"

"Abortion. She had an abortion. Man, I'm death on abortions! She knows that, the cunt!" Thinking about it all over again brought on some of the same feelings I'd had then.

"I started thinking about this baby boy—I'm sure it was a boy—and man, I lost it. I started drinking then, went out and bought a bottle of Jack and hit it hard. I'm thinking all kinds of things. You know, 'what coulda been' kinds of things. Me and her. Me and her and our baby boy. I just kinda went out of my skull. It probably didn't help I laid up in this motel room for three days doing nothing but slugging down Jack and going crazy in the head. That's when I did it."

I told him about the Norelco razor cord and it breaking

and all that stuff like I'd told Bud, only I hadn't told Bud exactly why I'd been in that motel room in the first place. I don't know why I was telling Manny all this. Maybe to get it all out, make me feel better. Only it didn't. Make me feel better, that is. I felt worse. I felt just like I had during those three days, only I didn't have any whiskey to help take the edge off. I know one thing—if I'd been on the bricks right that minute, I wouldn't be qualifying for any of those white poker chips they give out at A.A.

Time I went to bed that night I'd got it back under control somewhat. Only thing is I kept seeing Donna's fucking face and I hated the way I felt. Like I still wanted us to be together.

Ain't that some shit?

TWENTY-ONE

Wouldn't you know it? I start thinking about Donna again and what happens! What happens is that Mr. Bliss, one of the guards who worked the visiting room, sent a runner to the barber shop with a pass for me. I had a visitor.

Donna.

For a minute, I thought about refusing the visit. A stronger man would've. That wasn't me.

On the way up to the front, all kinds of weird things were going through my mind.

None of which, as it turned out, were even remotely close to reality.

"Jake," she said, once I sat in the chair across from her. I couldn't take my eyes off her. I didn't even want to blink for fear that this was all an apparition, that I'd wake up in my bunk holding my johnson with sweat pouring into my eyes.

She looked so fine. Women always look fine when you've been inside for a while. Even the dogs look like...*cute* dogs. All you see is a pussy and all pussies look beautiful. I swear, if the ugliest woman in the world sat across from me when I'd been locked up for a while, the only thing that would be on my mind would be how to cop a peek up her dress.

But Donna was gorgeous no matter where you saw her. I remember the first time I saw her without any makeup on and without thinking, I said, "You don't have any eyes!" She didn't. Well, at least not the eyes I was used to. Without mascara and the other goop she looked...*Swedish*. That's what I told her, after the shock of seeing her eyes naked had passed. "You look Swedish," I said, the master of originality. "Like Ingrid Bergman or something."

She had on her eye makeup today. Her hair was wild in that new way girls were doing it—"scrunched," I think they called it—and she had on a lemon-yellow dress that was working as hard as it could to keep her boobs from falling out of it. She was getting dirty looks from all the other women on her side of the chairs. Looks from the guys on my side, too, and they were dirty looks, too, only a different kind of dirty. All of a sudden, I wanted to fight every swinging dick in the room, while at the same time feeling so damned juiced with pride because of the drop-dead movie star that came to see *me*, I couldn't see straight. I knew every man Jack in that visiting room was going to be stroking the bald man that night in their cell...and I knew who every damn one of them was going to be picturing.

She looked like she'd gained a little weight, too, which was a good thing. Donna was always on some stupid diet or the other, always eating ExLax chunks like they were Almond Joys, or sticking her finger down her throat. She could throw up and never make a sound. Just a little *filip!* and it was gone. I watched her do it dozens of times and I swear her stomach never even moved.

I was always on her to gain some weight. Crack on her every chance I got. She subscribed to *Weight Watchers Magazine* and when it came in the mail, I'd bring it in from the mailbox and announce, "You got your *Hog Digest*. You make the centerfold this month?" She'd naturally get mad and I'd ask what the hell did she get stuff like that for.

"You look fantastic, babe. I always said you were too skinny."

She looked at me and got this funny look on her face.

"Well…that's why I came to see you, Jake."

About her weight? Shit, it looked good!

"I'm going have a baby, Jake."

I just sat there, a goofy grin spreading all over my entire face. I couldn't stop it. The worse I felt inside, as what she was saying sank in, the wider my grin got.

"You're pregnant?"

Yes she was. Twins. She'd already had one of those ultra sounds. Two boys. You could see their penises, she said. "You wanna see?" She reached for the envelop they'd let her bring in with her.

"That's all right," I said, waving my hand to stop her. That was the last thing I wanted to see. Ever.

"So," I said finally, after a long silence. "Why didn't you just write me a letter?"

"Oh, Jake!" She reached over, put her hand on my knee. I pushed it away. I wanted to just get up, leave, but I didn't.

"I'm getting married. Next Tuesday. I just…" She stopped, dabbed at her eyes with a Kleenex she must've had ready in her hand. "I just thought I should tell you in person. I owe you that much. We—"

I stood up, put up my hand like a traffic cop.

"There is no *we*, Donna." It was like that time at Alexander's. I knew I should say something memorable, something that would just reach up and bite her ass every time she thought about it, but I just couldn't think of a damn thing. I stood there and looked down at her and I saw the hack up at the podium start to come over, like he thought there was going to be trouble.

"Bye, Donna," I said. I turned and walked toward the turnkey who let inmates in and out for their visits.

TWENTY-TWO

Boles was back.

I was cutting a guy's hair when Manny came over and told me. He'd been up front, talking to the guard on duty that day. They put him in the infirmary. The guard thought he'd be there at least a week before they put him back out in the population and gave him limited duty. Probably put him in the library for a while, the guard told Manny. That made sense. Put an illiterate in charge of Pendleton's priceless Zane Grey paperback collection.

There was no question I had to get to him. It was obvious he hadn't snitched on me yet but I knew it was only a matter of time.

It's hard to move around in prison. In movies, it seems like guys come and go pretty much as they want. All they have to do is bribe a guard or some trusty. That might be the case in Tinseltown, but at Pendleton it was a different story. You couldn't take a crap without a pass. And what're you supposed to be bribing guards with? Packs of cigarettes? True, I had some green, over three hundred bucks, which made me practically a millionaire in here, but three thousand wouldn't be enough to bribe a guard into a situation where he might end up in here doing time with the guys he's been abusing. Cops who get busted are no big deal, but hacks? Ha! Hacks are a different story.

And that's another thing. Guards. In the flicks you've got

these hacks that are either James Cagney tough or a Bing Crosby type in the old movie "Boys Town," but one thing they all seem to be is smart. Hah! At Pendleton, the pay scale for officers was barely above minimum wage and you don't get Einsteins for that kind of money, generally. There was a standing joke that they recruited the hacks from among the bums that rode the rails, that jumped off that midnight train that rolled by every night. When the whistle blew, guys would yell out that the warden must be hiring. Most of them were borderline criminals themselves, and more than a few were downright sadistic. The average hack couldn't get a steady job in a 7-Eleven, mopping floors and stocking potato chips. Give them a uniform and badge and half an hour training on the firing range, and they're Super Cop in their little pinheaded minds. Worse than rent-a-cops.

Oh sure, there's one or two good ones. Like Jonesy. It was funny, though. The best hacks were almost always black. They were the opposite of the blacks who were incarcerated. I couldn't figure that out for the longest time, but now I think it's because this was the best job they could get because of their color, and inside they were decent people who took their jobs seriously. The white guards, though, they were the worst white guys out there, couldn't get a good job in spite of their color. So what you get is the best blacks and the worst whites got to be hacks, and the opposite of the guys they're guarding, the inmates.

And the white hacks were the most prejudiced people I ever knew. They were all the time cracking on the black guards. Not in front of them, of course, but in front of white inmates, they did it all the time. I never heard the black officers do the same.

Black and white are weird, the more you think about it. Just when you think all blacks are the same, up pops a Jonesy, who's a better man than any twenty white guys, and then there's white hacks like the Delaneys, who are pure assholes, somebody you wish would get caught out in the middle of the yard during the next riot by all the guys he's dropped a bench on.

The long and short of it, though, was I couldn't bribe a guard and get over to the infirmary where Boles was. I had to figure out something else, and it looked damned near impossible.

I was still trying to cook up a scheme when the situation changed three days later. For the better. Boles got released from the infirmary, and just like that guard had predicted, he was put in the library. Good news. He'd be much easier to get to, there. I just had to dope out a way to get there without getting caught. That meant I couldn't get a pass to the library since that'd leave a record on somebody's pass sheet.

The smart thing to do was get to Boles quick. He was still weak from his wounds. Also, he hadn't talked yet. If I waited too long he'd not only be stronger and harder to take down but he might have a change of heart and snitch me out.

I wished this was the movies. In the movies all those little technical difficulties wouldn't matter. Somehow, miraculously, I'd find myself alone with Boles and no one in the entire joint would know I was there. Like we can walk around wherever we want anytime we want! Right.

My man Dusty came through, though. Just like in the friggin' movies. Go figure.

"I got something for you," he said when we came in that night from chow.

"What?"

"You got to fix that guy over at the library, right?"

He knew I did.

"You told me you might need some help sometime with this guy."

I was surprised he remembered, and then I wasn't. Dusty was no lame-o.

"So what you got?"

"Here."

He put a piece of paper in my hand. It was a pass. "Free-walkin'" passes we called 'em. Only trusties got this kind of pass. It allowed you free movement wherever you wanted to go inside the walls. The best thing was it didn't have your name on it. A solid gold pass, especially for what I needed it for.

Dusty told me one other thing.

"Do it tomorrow morning," he said. I wanted to know why then. "'Cause, stupid, you're gonna need an alibi maybe, and I can give you one. I've got to take the barber shop towels over to the laundry and I'm going to ask for you to help me. You got twenty minutes to do it in. I got a buddy at the laundry I already talked to. He's gonna say you came in with me, dropped the laundry off."

It's things like this let you know who your friends are.

That night I had the weirdest dream. Practically every night I had a dream—nightmares most of the time—while I was behind bars. On the bricks I never dreamed. This one was about Donna. When we first hooked up Donna had gone off the deep end right away, was all over my case with phone calls and stuff, all the time telling me how much I drove her ass crazy. I was seeing lots of women then and wasn't pussywhipped over her at all. Oh, I liked her then and she was great in the sack and all, but I wasn't driven like I got later.

I was asleep in the dream—don't think about that—I did, and got a headache, and something wakes me up, and it's Donna. She's got this knife, and she's trying to cut off my johnson and I'm half-awake in the dream and probably in real life, too, and I'm holding her off when she drops the knife and I relax my grip on her hands and she rakes her fingernails across my face and I can't see, whether it's the blood from where her nails dinged me or because I'm not all the way awake, I don't know, and she's screaming at the top of her lungs, "If I can't have it nobody can!" I woke up because what I said to her got me to laughing, both in the dream itself and in waking, and then I knew I was awake, really awake, and I was laughing so hard I had tears. What I said in the dream was, "Does this mean we're not going to the prom together, honey?".

Bud was in there, in the dream, I forgot how, and a bunch of other stuff like you get in dreams, falling off cliffs and stuff. Dream stuff, who the fuck knows what it means.

That's when I woke up, my heart beating like I'd been doing amyl nitrate poppers and I'm laughing like somebody in the Squirrel Factory, and there was some fucker in the back of the dorm ripping out these horrible sobs.

I felt the sweat chill as I threw off my blanket. I yelled, "Somebody put a dick in that asshole's mouth!" I barefooted it over to the window and looked out, and the cooking crew was heading across the quad to the mess hall in their whites so I figured it was four-thirty since that's when they went over to start destroying breakfast.

There was no use trying to get back to sleep. They'd be rousting us for wakeup in another hour, anyway, so I went and got my shaving gear and took a shower and shaved, brushed my teeth. Nice, I thought. You could actually take a shit without ten thousand guys screaming six feet from you. I'd have to remember that and get up early from now on.

I sat on the stool longer than what I needed, just thinking. About the dream and Donna and Boles and all kinds of shit like that. Just sat there getting madder and madder. It wasn't like I was building a hard-on so's I could jack up Boles, later on. I never needed that shit. You know, get mad so I could jump on somebody. That kind of shit's for punks. The best way is to not even think about it. Just do it.

That's the best way to do anything major. 'Specially when you got a choice, got two roads you can take. Like I could whack out Boles or I could do something else. Like nothing. Just not do it at all, see what happened then.

Fuck that. Boles was going down. I couldn't believe a guy could get stabbed that many times and still live. What was he, some kind of vampire? Thirty-some holes this punk gets with a laundry pin and he's over working in the library like he just got over the flu. I shoulda put a wooden stake through his motherfucking heart is what I shoulda done, prevented all this happy horseshit.

It's like a stickup. Most outlaws I talked to got busted 'cause they plan too much. Figure out what to do if this happens, that happens. The best way is not even know you're gonna do it till it happens. Like, you're in a supermarket, buying some gum, whatever, and on the way out you see all the checkout girls heading with their money trays to the office on account of the next shift is there. Before you walked in, robbing somebody maybe was the last thing on your mind. You see that, all them trays stacked up on the desk in the office, the safe open and the smartest thing you can do is walk over, pull out your piece and tell the guy in the bowtie to bag it up, hand it over. Zip, boom, bang, you're out of the place and cruising down the road before you even know what you did. Just like that.

I never once in my entire life got caught on a job when I did it like that. The ones I keep getting busted on are the ones where you cased and planned and schemed for eleventeen years before and always—*always*—the one little thing you never thought of happens, and the next thing you know is you're trying to wipe black ink off your fingers with that one little paper towel they always give you, and you feel you're waking up from a bad dream. Into one that's worse.

I'm thinking all this and then I just did it. Dropped a sheet over all them other thoughts about Donna and even Boles and just went into another part of my mind.

We were walking out of the dorm after breakfast and Manny was saying something to me. In fact, he was almost screaming before I noticed anything.

"What?" I said, wondering why he was yelling at me, and then Dusty, who was walking with us, said, "Leave him alone, Manny. He's in the zone."

He gave me a look and took a quick glance around, and then his hand touched mine and I knew what it was. I slipped it into my shirt. Without looking I could feel it was a knife, a regular hunting knife, not some piece of shit that had been jury-rigged from a piece of metal from one of the shops. This was a serious killing weapon. What he did, what I had in my hand, registered, not in the front part of my mind but in the back, where I was.

We got to the barber school and I just went on back to stand behind my chair instead of screwing around with the others. A couple of the guys walked by, said something, and I just nodded. I didn't have a clue what they said to me.

Then Mr. Dillsie came to the door of his office and yelled at me to come up front, help Dusty with the towels. I could see Dusty behind the glass. There were five large sacks. I grabbed three of them and Dusty the other two, and we went out the back door.

"Run," Dusty hissed, once we were out of sight of the school. "You gotta book, man!"

We ran all the way to the laundry and his man was standing outside waiting for us. "You got fifteen minutes, maybe twenty," Dusty said. "Go!"

I threw down my sacks and took off again, heading up toward the quad, around the chow hall, and luck was with me. I didn't pass a single guard, only one inmate. I kept my head down and I don't think the guy even noticed me. The library was two buildings down from the chow hall and nobody was on the walk in front of me. Clear sailing. This was the best time. There shouldn't be anybody else in the library, except for the librarian, for at least another hour.

There wasn't.

I went in quick, closed the door behind me. I could feel the knife where I'd put it under my shirt, the handle stuck down behind my belt.

At first, I thought nobody was there, and then I heard something, sounded like a book drop, back in the office. I walked back and went into the room. He was there, bending over. He straightened up, a book in his hand and looked at me.

TWENTY-THREE

"Boles," I said. I could see the fear in his eyes.

"I didn't snitch you out, man," he said, laying the book down on the desk in front of him and stepping back. He moved kind of stiff-like, and I guess I would, too, I had that many holes in me.

"I know. I couldn't be here if you had, could I."

I pulled out my knife.

"Why you gonna do this?"

"You know why."

He took another step back and was up against the wall. I started toward him.

"Oh, man." His voice broke. He put his hands up, palms facing me and began edging along the wall toward the door. "Man, you're safe. I'm not going to tell who shanked me. If I was gonna tell I would have already done it. I'm sorry for what I did to you. We're even. Don't you see we're even?"

In a way, he was right. I'd had the same thought myself. The pain I'd put him through almost certainly matched what he'd done to me. In one way the score was settled.

I didn't even feel the same anger I had when he'd raped me. The day I'd shanked him up on the laundry roof it had disap-peared, vanishing a little bit with every hole I put in him until it was all gone. There was no revenge left in my heart, none at all. It was just pure-d empty of everything, all malice.

I walked over to him and he just stood there. I don't think his knees would let him move. His eyes told me that. I stopped inches from him. His hands went down to his sides.

"You won't talk? Ever?"

"Oh, man! No! I swear t'God! You're safe, man. I just want to do my time, get the fuck out of here, that's all."

I believed him. I could hear it in his voice.

"You don't even know my name, do you?" I said.

"No." He was telling the truth.

"My name's Jake Mayes," I said. Then I stabbed him. Who knows why? Just like that. It started in easy enough, then hit something solid so that I had to push harder on the handle before it went all the way in. I looked him in the eyes the whole time. It seemed like it lasted for hours, us standing there, and his eyes changed, just the least little bit, in realization of what was happening, I guess, and his eyelids started to quiver like he was trying to keep from blinking, as if once he blinked it was all over, and then all the bones just seemed to go out of his face. I reached up with my other hand, grabbed his shirt and eased him on down to the floor. His eyes were still open. He hadn't blinked but he was dead.

When I turned to walk away, the damndest thing happened. My back tooth hurt like hell and when I felt it with my tongue I knew why. It had bust clean in two. Man! Talk about something smarting! Instantly, I knew what had happened. It was the same tooth I'd chipped the last time I was in here, over to the chow hall. That time when the inmate mess cook buried the cleaver in the dude's stomach.

The next day I'd gone to the worthless third-world dentist over at the infirmary and he'd given me half a shot of Novocain and did a patch job of sorts on it. Musta been a better job than I thought, to last all this time. I guess I bit down kinda hard on it when I stuck Boles.

Reason I know the fucking dentist only gave me half a shot was I could feel every twitch he made with his stinking fingers and tools inside my mouth and I also knew why he'd been stingy with the juice. Bastard was getting rich selling shit like that to inmates who weren't particular about what kind of crap they ran in their veins.

Thinking about that made me remember that jerk Larry, betting me I'd be back.

Whoa. I was walking toward the library door when that hit me. Motherfuck! I hate it when an asshole like that turns out to be right. And he was. All of a sudden I knew just how right he was. I'd been on my way back here before I'd ever left. I stood there and thought about what that meant for a minute or two, and then it struck me that it wasn't the smartest thing in the world to do—hang around a room with a dead body—so I made tracks on out of there.

I got back to the laundry and Dusty was still there talking with his friend. I knew I had been gone longer than I should have.

"What you doing?" Dusty said, when I came up. "You're walking like you got all the time in the world, moron. C'mon, let's get the fuck out of here."

The other guy turned and went back inside the laundry and we started walking back to the barber school. On the way, Dusty asked me questions. "You get rid of the knife? Anybody see you?"

Back at the school I had a customer waiting for me. Dusty did, too. The guy wanted a flattop. I got out the triple-ought blade, rinsed it in the sterilizing solution. When I got done, I stepped back and looked. It was the best flattop I had ever cut. It was a fucking masterpiece, it was. You could land a plane on that flattop. I just laid down my clippers when the steam whistle blew. I knew what that meant. I looked over at

Dusty, and he at me, and he held his hand down low so nobody else could see and gave me a thumbs up. I just nodded. Ice-cold, that's the way I felt. Frosty. Peaceful. When that whistle blew, something happened inside. Time, as a concept, just disappeared. Just blew away in the wind, went over the wall. History...just like that tooth.

A couple of months later, Bud came down and Dusty got him into K Dorm with us. It was Kimmie he'd killed, but he told us it was an accident. She was giving him some grief, yakking that he was always out too late, lame crap like that, and he'd tapped her.

"I didn't even hit her that hard," he said. "I hit her lots harder lots of times. It was just a freak accident."

"Fucking life's a freak accident," I said, and we all laughed, me, him, Dusty and Manny. We were all outside on the ball field, sitting at one of the picnic tables, eating Oreos and smoking tightrolls, playing dominos.

This was as good as it gets, I thought, looking around. I saw a bird fly up to the wall and then it was gone, flew over the side. That was all right, I thought. Good fucking riddance. This was okay, too, sitting out in the grass with my buds. The green, green grass of home. No fucking broads hassling us, just good friends sitting around, having us a ball. I started to think of Donna but got that shit out of my mind. Thinking about broads is what fucks up your time in here. All I want to do now is my time.

Eight more years, thanks to Boles. Yeah, they found out it was me. Fuck it. Like I give a shit.

I can do eight years standing on my head.

Got my shit together, now. I could do eight times eight, snooze all the way through the whole thing. In the zone, man; I'm in the zone. You're in the zone, you're free. Fuck, you're freer than free. You're a man nobody fucks with. You're the fucking Master of the Universe. People step aside when you walk by. You stare at any motherfucker you want, all day long, you feel like it. Cracks me up, way these chumps try and become invisible, they see me coming down the tier walk.

Invisible *this*, I say in my head, when I walk by, and then I do whatever the fuck I want, whatever I feel like doing. Just what-the-fuck-ever. *Just like that*, amigo.

ABOUT THE AUTHOR

Les Edgerton is an ex-con, matriculating at Pendleton Reformatory in the sixties for burglary (plea-bargained down from multiple counts of burglary, armed robbery, strong-armed robbery and possession with intent). He was an outlaw for many years and was involved in shootouts, knifings, robberies, high-speed car chases, dealt and used drugs, was a pimp, worked for an escort service, starred in porn movies, was a gambler, served four years in the Navy, and had other misadventures.

He's since taken a vow of poverty (became a writer) with nineteen books in print. Three of his novels have been sold to German publisher Pulpmaster for the German language rights. His memoir, *Adrenaline Junkie*, is currently being marketed. Work of his has been nominated for or won: the Pushcart Prize, O. Henry Award, Edgar Allan Poe Award (short story category), Derringer Award, PEN/Faulkner Award, Jesse Jones Book Award, Spinetingler Magazine Award for Best Novel (Legends category), and the Violet Crown Book Award, among others. Screenplays of his have placed as a semifinalist in the Nicholl's and as a finalist in the Best of Austin and Writer's Guild's competitions.

He holds a B.A. from I.U. and the MFA in Writing from Vermont College. He was the writer-in-residence for three years at the University of Toledo, for one year at Trine University, and taught writing classes for UCLA, St. Francis University, Phoenix College, Writer's Digest, Vermont College, the New York Writer's Workshop and other places. He currently teaches a private novel-writing class online. He lives in Ft. Wayne, Indiana, where he immigrated to some years ago from the U.S. and is currently learning the language and customs there. He writes because he hates...a lot... Injustice and bullying are what he hates the most.

lesedgertononwriting.blogspot.com
lesedgerton.net
Twitter — @HookedOnNoir
Facebook — les.edgerton

OTHER TITLES FROM DOWN AND OUT BOOKS

See www.DownAndOutBooks.com for complete list

By Jerry Kennealy
Screen Test
Polo's Long Shot

By Dana King
Worst Enemies
Grind Joint
Resurrection Mall

By Ross Klavan, Tim O'Mara
and Charles Salzberg
Triple Shot

By S.W. Lauden
Crosswise
Crossed Bones

By Paul D. Marks and
Andrew McAleer (editor)
Coast to Coast vol. 1
Coast to Coast vol. 2

By Gerald O'Connor
The Origins of Benjamin Hackett

By Gary Phillips
The Perpetrators
Scoundrels (Editor)
Treacherous
3 the Hard Way

By Thomas Pluck
Bad Boy Boogie

By Tom Pitts
Hustle
American Static

By Robert J. Randisi
Upon My Soul
Souls of the Dead
Envy the Dead

By Charles Salzberg
Devil in the Hole
Swann's Last Song
Swann Dives In
Swann's Way Out

By Scott Loring Sanders
Shooting Creek and Other Stories

By Ryan Sayles
The Subtle Art of Brutality
Warpath
Let Me Put My Stories In You

By John Shepphird
The Shill
Kill the Shill
Beware the Shill

By James R. Tuck (editor)
Mama Tried vol. 1
Mama Tried vol. 2 (*)

By Lono Waiwaiole
Wiley's Lament
Wiley's Shuffle
Wiley's Refrain
Dark Paradise
Leon's Legacy

By Nathan Walpow
The Logan Triad

(*)—Coming Soon